FINAL SHOWDOWN

Maddux waited until he saw his men in place on the roof.

"Stay here and cover me," the ex-lawman said to Wilkes. "I'm going to get closer and draw them out."

The wounded Pinkerton agent grimaced from his shoulder wound as he grabbed his gun.

Maddux took a deep breath and ran out from behind the trough they were using for cover.

Running diagonally, he fired on the move, taking down one man. He headed for a doorway as the rooftop shooters opened up with a hurricane of hot lead.

As Maddux reloaded, he saw several of the outlaws fall, their guns firing wildly into the air. But through the clouds of gray gunsmoke, he noticed a big man running toward the livery. "The yella bastard's trying to get away!" he shouted to his men. "Keep them pinned down, and I'll get him!"

BACKSHOOTER

Robert J. Randisi

LEISURE BOOKS NEW YORK CITY

To Dale Walker,
from one Sutphen boy to another.

A LEISURE BOOK®

February 2005

Published by

Dorchester Publishing Co., Inc.
200 Madison Avenue
New York, NY 10016

Copyright © 1990 by Robert Randisi

ISBN 0-8439-5339-X

The name "Leisure Books" and the stylized "L" with design are trademarks of Dorchester Publishing Co., Inc.

Printed in the United States of America.

Visit us on the web at www.dorchesterpub.com.

BACKSHOOTER

Prologue

I

Maddux was in a bad position.

In fact, this was as bad a spot as he'd found himself in in a long time.

He was lying on his back in a gully. He was holding his gun in his left hand, because he was carrying a bullet in his right arm. There were three men out there who wanted nothing better than to kill him after first stringing him up to a tree.

He didn't know why two of them were so mad. He was only after Lucas Freeling. Unfortunately, Freeling's friends were loyal to Lucas, who was a rapist and a killer. Maddux wondered how a man like that could command loyalty—unless the other two were just as bad as he was.

He'd tracked Lucas Freeling and his friends for over a hundred miles, and they had probably gotten pretty damned tired of him dogging their trail. So they'd lain in wait for him here, and before he knew it there was a bullet in his right arm and he was lying on the ground, his horse having reared at the sound of the first shot.

Actually, the horse rearing had probably saved his life, because the two subsequent shots had sailed harmlessly over his head as he was falling off his horse.

He had rolled immediately, coming to a stop on his back in the gully. He'd pulled his gun out right-handed and switched it to his left. His right hand was already starting to go numb, which could have meant that there was some serious damage done to his right arm.

Using his bandana he tied off the wound in his arm as well as he could, enough to staunch the flow of blood for a while at least.

Now he had to concentrate on getting out of this situation alive.

Lucas Freeling narrowed his eyes as he peered toward the gully that Maddux had scampered into.

"Did you see him roll into that gully?" he asked the others. "He's hit bad."

"Let's go in and finish him off, Lucas," Harve Morrow said.

Freeling looked at both Morrow and Slim Drake.

"I want that lawman alive, boys," Freeling said. "I'm gonna hang him up by his balls as a message to other lawmen."

"Wouldn't the message get across just as well if we killed him?" Drake asked.

"We'll kill him," Freeling said, "when he begs for it."

Both Morrow and Drake had winced when Freeling mentioned hanging Maddux up . . . that way. No man, they thought, deserved to have that done to him. If they'd ever needed further proof that Lucas Freeling was a cruel, heartless bastard, this was it. More than loyalty *to* Lucas Freeling, they responded to their fear *of* him.

"All right, Lucas," Drake said, "if that's the way you want it."

"That's the way I want it."

"How do we get him out of that gully then?" Morrow asked.

"He'll come out on his own," Freeling said. "He's hit bad, so he's gonna have to try to get away. All we have to do is wait."

Maddux had one major advantage, and one major disadvantage. He wasn't sure that one successfully offset the other, but they were both there and he had to examine them.

His disadvantage was the fact that he was wounded. He couldn't afford to wait them out, because he was the one who was losing blood. Freeling would surely be content to wait him out, biding his time until Maddux made his move to escape.

His advantage was the fact that Freeling wanted him alive. He'd shouted as much to him just moments after he'd crawled into the gully. Maddux had winced at the thought.

Still, when *you* were willing to kill someone, while *they* were trying to take you alive, *that* was an advantage.

"What do you got against this lawman?" Drake asked Freeling.

Freeling looked at Drake, then at Morrow. Both men were watching him curiously. They'd been waiting an hour now, and maybe they weren't criticizing him, maybe they just wanted to talk.

"Let me tell you about this bastard," Freeling said. "He's killed three of my old partners, three good men who could take almost any man face to face—except Maddux. Now he's been on my trail for better'n a hundred miles, and I'm gettin' damned tired of looking over my shoulder."

"Who were your three partners?"

"Joe Santos, Kenny Muldoon, and Whip Wilcox."

"Didn't they call him Kid Whip?" Drake asked.

"They did," Freeling said, "until Maddux killed him."

"You rode with those three?" Morrow asked.

"I did, and he killed them," Freeling said. "He's not gonna kill me. I'm gonna do something those three couldn't do. I'm gonna kill me a lawman named Maddux." He looked at them again and said, "You know what killin' him is gonna do for me?"

"Make you famous," Drake said.

"It sure as hell is," Freeling said, "but taking him alive, torturing him, and *then* killing him is gonna make me *in*-famous."

"What's *in*-famous?" Morrow asked, frowning.

"That's when you're more than famous," Freeling said, "and that's just what I'm gonna be."

Privately, Drake and Morrow wondered if being present when he did it would make them in-famous as well.

Maddux woke with a start.

Jesus, had he really fallen asleep? If he ever needed proof that this game was for younger men, this was it. His wife kept telling him that this was no business for a man nearing fifty. For once he was thinking that maybe she was right.

He turned and peered out to see if the three men were still there. One shot was fired, just to let him know they were still there.

Christ, they could have walked right up on him while he was asleep.

Maddux tried to move his right arm and found that it had stiffened up on him. He passed his left hand over his eyes and forehead and it came away wet. There was heat throbbing behind his eyes and he knew he had a high fever.

He had to get out of there and get some medical treatment. He stood to lose the arm, or his life, if he didn't get help—that is, if he didn't get killed trying to get away.

Get away? Shit!

He was thinking about getting away from these three when he should have been thinking about a way to get them. If word got out that they had gotten away from him—that *he* had gotten away from *them*—he'd lose all the respect he'd built up over the years. In this business that respect—that *fear*—could mean the difference between living and dying.

Maddux finally decided that he had little to lose and a lot to gain. If he died, he died. It had to happen to everyone at one time or another. But this time wasn't what he had in mind.

"What the—" Morrow said.

He'd been watching while Freeling and Drake sat with their backs to him. Now Freeling turned at the sound of his voice.

"What is it?"

"You'd better look at this, Lucas."

Freeling got up onto his knees and peered over the

11

rocks they were using for cover.

"What the—" he said.

What he saw was Maddux standing up in plain sight, holding his gun jammed underneath his chin. He looked for all the world like he was gonna blow his own head off.

"What the hell is he doing?" Drake asked.

"What's it look like," Freeling said. "He's gonna steal my moment from me. If he kills himself I'll never be *in*-famous."

Freeling started to stand up, and both Morrow and Drake said, "What are you doing?"

"I'm gonna talk to him."

Freeling moved out from behind the rocks, his gun holstered.

"Maddux, what the hell do you think you're doin'?" he demanded.

"What does it look like I'm doing, Freeling?" Maddux asked. "I don't relish begging to die, and I don't think I can get away from you. Not in the condition I'm in. So I guess I'll just blow my own head off."

"Don't do that!" Freeling said.

Behind him both Morrow and Drake moved out from behind the rocks, watching.

"What do you care?" Maddux asked. "I'll be dead and off your trail."

"I want the pleasure of killing you myself," Freeling said. "You ain't gonna steal that from me, Maddux."

"Watch me."

"No, wait!"

"What are you going to do?" Maddux said. "Stop me by killing me?"

"I'll make a deal with you," Freeling said.

"What kind of deal?"

"I'll kill you quick," Freeling said.

"You'll kill me quick?"

"Yeah."

"Shit," Maddux said, "I can do that myself."

As Maddux's finger tightened on the trigger of his gun, Freeling shouted, "No!" and started forward.

As Freeling charged him—obviously intending to try and stop him from blowing his own head off—Maddux lowered the gun and pointed it at the man.

"What—" Freeling said, trying to stop his forward motion.

"I changed my mind," Maddux said, and squeezed the trigger.

Morrow and Drake, seeing Freeling shot down, decided that it would be best for them to get out of there.

Maddux watched as the two men ran for their horses, mounted, and rode off. Then he went over to Freeling's body and nudged it with the toe of his boot.

"Lucky for me," he said, "that you had more guts than brains."

Maddux turned his back on the downed man and moved to take a step, but his legs would no longer hold him. Suddeny, he felt as if he were floating. He heard a shot and felt a sharp pain in his back. He didn't even feel it when his face hit the dirt.

One

The pain was back.

No, Kyle Maddux thought as he straightened up, that wasn't exactly right. The pain was *always* there; some days it was just worse than others.

Today was just one of those days.

"What are you doing, Kyle?"

He turned and knew that the look on his face was one of guilt as he stared at his wife, Laura. Now in her early forties, Laura was still a handsome woman. When he looked at her he could still see the woman he'd married more than fourteen years ago. He would still never know what such a woman saw in a man ten years her senior. Back then Laura's hair had been black as the wings of a raven. Now there were streaks of gray in it, but he didn't care. When they walked down the street in town he saw that she still commanded admiring looks from other men, and he was proud of her.

He was also a little afraid of her, but what husband isn't a little afraid of his wife? The man who said he wasn't was a liar.

15

"We need wood," he said lamely.

"That's what Shadoweyes is here for, Kyle Maddux!" she said, scolding him. "Now put down that ax—your back hurts, doesn't it?"

He could never hide it from her.

"It aches a bit," he admitted, dropping the ax to the ground.

"Come inside," she said. "I've made some coffee."

He smiled and followed her into the house.

The town of Cromwell had given them this piece of land and the house, after he had recovered from the wounds he'd received while chasing down Lucas Freeling. It was lucky for him that his deputy back then had been almost as stubborn as he was. Joe Hannibal had trailed Maddux while Maddux was trailing Freeling. If Hannibal hadn't found him he probably would have died from those wounds. He owed Joe a lot, and one of the things he did was endorse Hannibal for his job when he'd retired, three years ago.

The house was as it was three years ago, built of fine pine lumber, with three rooms. The bank had taken it over when the old owner had died, and would have sold it had they not turned it over to the Madduxes. The banker, Charles Timberlane, had come up with the idea of giving it to Kyle and Laura in gratitude for the twelve years that Kyle had been marshal there, and the rest of the town council had gone along with it.

Kyle sat down at the table and Laura put a steaming cup of coffee in front of him.

"You didn't sleep very well last night, did you?" she asked.

"I tossed some," he said, looking into the coffee cup.

"Did you have the dream?"

16

Yes, he'd had the dream. It was amazing how he was always able to feel the impact of the bullet, and the pain, over and over again in The Dream.

The thing that really bothered him was that he never knew who had shot him. When Joe Hannibal had found him, he and Lucas Freeling were lying on the ground, both looking good and dead. Freeling *had been* dead but, by some miracle, Maddux had still been alive. It was even more of a miracle that he'd survived the trek back to the nearest town, being dragged on a litter behind Hannibal's horse.

"Maybe Freeling lived long enough to plug you one more," Hannibal had said at the time, but Maddux always doubted it. He had shot Freeling, and he'd been certain the man was dead. Those other two who were riding with him—it was possible that one of them had sneaked back and done the deed, but he doubted that too. When they'd lit out they'd looked like they'd never want to come back.

"I had the dream." He hated admitting it to her. He took the dream as a sign of weakness.

He appreciated that Laura did not fuss over him. Instead she simply asked him if he'd like a piece of pie with the coffee, and he said yes.

When she had placed the hunk of apple pie in front of him he said, "I think I'll take a ride into town after this."

"What for?" she asked.

"I need some tobacco," he said, which was true, but not the real reason. He just felt he needed to get away for a while, have a beer, maybe see Joe Hannibal.

"Well, take the buckboard," she said. "You know your back can't take you sitting a horse anymore."

Little did she know that he sometimes sneaked away just to ride again.

17

"I'll take the buckboard," he promised, and hacked off a piece of that pie.

The town council had given Ben Tibbs some trouble when he'd first put up the sign bearing the name of his saloon. In the beginning the sign had said HORSE'S ASS SALOON and it had had a big horse's hind section hanging right over the entrance. But the women of the town had started to complain to the council, and the council had taken it up with Tibbs, who'd reluctantly agreed to move the horse's ass inside-"With all the *other* horse's asses"—where it now hung over the bar.

Maddux always figured that he'd put the horse's ass on the outside in the first place just so he'd have something to bargain with when the complaining started.

And it worked like a charm.

Maddux entered the saloon and went directly to the bar. Sam Waters was tending bar as usual, and gave him a surprised look.

"What brings you to town, Marshal?" Most of the people in town still called him Marshal. He had protested at first, but had decided that if Presidents can stand to be addressed by their former title, who was he to complain?"

"Supplies," Maddux said, "and a cold mug of beer."

"I can help you there," Waters said, and drew Maddux a cold one.

Sam was a tall, emaciated-looking man in his mid-fifties. He worked the day shift in the saloon. The night shift belonged to Dog Nichols. Dog was six and a half feet tall and almost as wide, and was able to handle the rougher shift more effectively than Sam.

A door in the back wall opened, and Ben Tibbs stepped out. When he saw Maddux he sauntered over to the bar.

Tibbs was a gambler, and a fancy dresser. A man in his mid-thirties, he had an eye for the ladies, and the eye was usually returned. In the six months since he'd opened the saloon, Maddux had become friends with Tibbs and Sam Waters. He was still working on Dog Nichols, who had the disposition of a three-legged dog. His name was actually Doug, but where he'd grown up everyone had pronounced it "Dog" and it had stuck.

"Afternoon, Marshal," Tibbs said.

"Ben." Maddux looked up at the stuffed horse's ass hanging over the bar and said, "I don't know how you manage to keep the flies away from that thing."

"I just charm them away, Marshal," Tibbs said, smiling.

Looking at Tibbs's best smile, Maddux could believe it. He'd seen many women charmed by that smile, even when they disapproved of Ben's profession.

"How's the ranch coming?" Tibbs asked.

"It's coming along."

"Did you ever hire any help?"

"Got a feller helping me."

"Oh? Anyone I know?"

Maddux hesitated and then said, "John Shadoweyes."

"The breed?" Sam Waters asked. "He'll rob you blind, Maddux—"

"John's a good man, Sam," Maddux said. "All he needs is a chance."

"And you're giving it to him, huh?" Tibbs asked.

"Someone's got to."

"You know, another time you might have been

19

hunting John Shadoweyes," Tibbs said.

"Well, this isn't another time, is it?" he said.

"No, it damned sure isn't," Tibbs said. "If it was, I'd be standing in my own place in Portsmouth Square, San Francisco, that's for damned sure."

Ever since Maddux had met Tibbs, the man had talked about owning his own place in Portsmouth Square.

"That beer's on the house, Marshal," Tibbs said. "Sam, he pays for the second one. All right?"

"That's fair," Maddux said.

Tibbs slapped him on the shoulder and said, "I've got a little filly waiting."

"That's no surprise," Maddux said to Waters as Tibbs walked out. "Is this one married?"

Waters shrugged and said, "I don't rightly know which one he's got waiting, but there's a fifty-fifty chance that she is."

"He might get shot by a jealous husband long before he ever gets to Portsmouth Square," Maddux said.

"That's the truth."

Maddux made some more small talk with Sam until he finished his beer, and then declined to take a second one.

"I'll tell Ben you had your free one and took a walk," Sam said.

"Tell him I'll be back later," Maddux said.

When Maddux left the saloon he headed for the marshal's office to visit with Joe Hannibal. Joe had been Maddux's deputy for five years. All during that time they had maintained a relationship of marshal and deputy. Since Maddux's retirement, however, they had become friends.

As Maddux entered the office Hannibal was at his coffee pot, which was where he spent a lot of time.

"That stuff is going to kill you one of these days," Maddux said.

"Coffee?"

"*Your* coffee."

"In that case," Hannibal said, "I'll pour you one so I don't die alone."

Hannibal turned with two cups in his hands and Maddux accepted one. Hannibal sat behind his desk and Maddux took a seat across from him.

"What brings you to town?"

"Tobacco."

Hannibal was in his late thirties, not tall, and very powerfully built. When he'd first laid eyes on him, Maddux had likened him to a bear, and had seen no reason in the ensuing years to change his mind. Hannibal had a short beard and a deep, drawling voice. His brutish appearance belied the sharp mind he possessed, and usually made people underestimate him.

"What else have you got on your mind?" Hannibal asked as Maddux sipped the coffee.

"What makes you think I've got something else on my mind?" Maddux asked.

"Because you really only brave my coffee when you've had the dream and want to talk about it."

Maddux was in the middle of another sip, and made a face. He leaned forward and put the cup down on Hannibal's desk. "You're right, I had the dream," he said, "but I don't want to talk about it."

"Fine," Hannibal said. "We'll talk about something else."

"What are you reading there?" Maddux asked. Hannibal had the newspaper opened on his desk.

"Ah, I'm reading about this Backshooter varmint."

"Did he kill someone else?"

"Yep," Hannibal said.

"Where this time?"

"A little town just this side of the Rio Grande."

"He must be taking his act into Mexico."

"Yeah, well, they can have him," Hannibal said, closing the paper.

"Let me see it," Maddux said.

"What for?" Hannibal said, holding the now-folded newspaper. "It's all the old stuff."

"Let me see it," Maddux asked, again.

Hannibal sighed and handed Maddux the paper. Maddux immediately turned to the Backshooter article and started reading it.

"You're becoming obsessed with this thing, Kyle," Hannibal said.

Maddux didn't answer, but Hannibal knew he was right. Ever since the Backshooter had claimed his third victim, Kyle Maddux had taken an interest in the case. Now that the man's list of kills was up to an even dozen in a two-year period, Hannibal was afraid of what Kyle Maddux might do.

"Kyle—"

"Shh."

Hannibal leaned over and slammed his pawlike hand down on the newspaper.

"What the—"

"Just because we never found who shot you in the back doesn't mean it was this fella."

"It's a possibility," Maddux said.

"This fella didn't claim his first victim until more than a year after you were shot."

"What if *I* was his first victim, only nobody knows it?" Maddux asked.

"There could be *hundreds* of victims before his acknowledged first," Hannibal said, "but that still doesn't mean you're one of them."

Kyle frowned and looked away from his friend.

"You know this is getting to be an obsession," Hannibal said, "and you know where it's going to lead."

"Where?"

"I know you, Kyle," Hannibal said. "Retirement hasn't set well with you. You're looking for an excuse to get up on a horse and go looking for this jasper."

"Bull," Maddux said, but even to him his tone sounded unconvincing.

"Sure," Hannibal said, "it's bull." The marshal leaned forward and said, "I'll bet if I searched your house I'd come up with a map of this fella's movements. Am I right? Huh?"

"Damn you," Maddux said, "you're too damned smart, Joe Hannibal."

"I learned from you, Kyle," Hannibal said. "I learned to know my subjects."

"You been studying on me?"

"I've been watching you, my friend," Hannibal said, "and I'm gonna keep on watching you."

"You do that, *friend*," Maddux said, "and you're going to get pretty bored."

They sat in silence for a few moments, and then Hannibal said, "You still got that breed working for you?"

"John Shadoweyes? Yeah, why?"

"If you knew how many times I've had him in a cell for—"

"He's not drinking anymore," Maddux said.

"He's gone off the bottle before, Maddux, and he's gone right back on again."

Maddux shrugged. "He's good with horses."

"When he's sober."

"I guess we'll just have to wait and see. I'm not losing anything by giving the man a job."

23

"He gets real violent when he drinks," Hannibal said, warningly.

"So I'll watch him," Maddux said, standing up. "Come on, let's go over to the hotel and get some real coffee."

"You buying?"

"Since when did a lawman buy?" Maddux said. "Of course I'm buying."

As they left his office Hannibal said, "You know what you need?"

"What?"

"A woman."

"In case you forgot, Joe, I have a woman."

"No, I mean a younger woman," Hannibal said. "Somebody to take your mind off of things."

"You got somebody in mind?"

"Sure," Hannibal said. "Susan, over at the hotel."

"Stop playing cupid, Joe," Maddux said. "Susan is a nice girl, and a good waitress."

"That's my point," Hannibal said. "I mean, that she's a nice girl."

Maddux waved his hand at Hannibal in a "shut up," gesture and walked ahead.

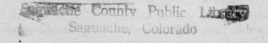
24

Two

Sue Daniels saw Maddux as soon as he entered the hotel dining room, and hurried over to his table.

"Hi, Kyle."

Maddux looked up at Sue, struck as usual by her freshfaced beauty. She was blonde and had a peaches-and-cream complexion. She was twenty-eight, old enough for him to notice her all the time, but young enough for him to do nothing more.

On the way over to the hotel someone had called out to Joe Hannibal, who had told Maddux to go on ahead and get a table.

"Hello, Susan."

"Would you like to order now?"

"I'm, uh, waiting for Marshal Hannibal."

"Does he know you're in here?"

"Yes, he knows."

"Coffee while you wait?"

"Yes, thank you."

He watched her walk away, admiring the way her behind looked in her dress, and then chiding himself for being a lecherous old man. She was, after all, about twenty-five years younger than he was—give or take a year. He loved Laura and would never do

25

anything to hurt her, but Sue Daniels's attentions whenever he came to town boosted his ego in a way that he sometimes needed.

He hoped he never had to explain *that* to Laura.

The dining room was doing a brisk business as it was dinnertime, and almost all of the tables were taken by this time. Maddux knew that, despite the fact that she was very busy, he'd be getting Susan's very best service.

After almost three years it still felt odd not to have his gun on his hip, not having to shift every so often to accommodate it. He was grateful, however, that in his new life he didn't have to carry it anymore.

He was thinking about that when he saw the two men enter. They moved through the doorway from the lobby to the dining room and stopped. It appeared that they were looking for a table, but there was something about them that alerted Maddux. Later, he'd be surprised that the old instinct for survival had not gone stale in retirement, but right then he didn't have time to think about that.

He could see things developing very clearly. Sue was on her way to his table with his coffee, and another waitress was moving toward the two men to see if she could help them. Maddux was seated just about in the center of the dining room, with people behind him, in front of him, and on both sides.

The potential of the situation couldn't have been worse.

He sat watching the two men, peripherally aware of the movement of the two women. He forgot everything else in the room, all the idle chatter and clinking of glasses and silverware. Perspiration broke out on his brow, and he was trying to think of a way out when the two men moved.

Sue had reached him by this time and was saying,

"Here's your coffee—"

"Down, Sue!" he shouted.

"Wha—"

"Get . . . down!" he shouted, pushing her.

The two men saw him moving and the one on the right—the left-handed one—would have had him if it wasn't for the other waitress. She reached them and put her hand on the man's left arm, saying, "Can I help—"

Angrily, the man pushed her away from him, and it delayed his move to his gun.

The other man just wasn't very fast.

By the time both men had their guns out, Maddux had overturned the table and had it in front of him, at the same time yelling, "Everybody down!"

Everyone in the place looked up as he shouted, and then the shooting started and screams of fear and cries of pain began.

Maddux felt the table jolt as each slug pounded into it, and knew he had to do something before an innocent bystander got killed. He grabbed a table leg in each hand, lifted the whole table, and ran towards the two men, screaming at the top of his lungs.

The table shook in his grasp as they continued to fire, and then suddenly the firing stopped as they ran out of bullets.

He ran into them then, ramming them both with the table and forcing them back into the lobby, where they went sprawling. He tossed the chewed-up table away and charged them.

He pulled one man to his feet and hit him in the face, then turned to find the second man up on one knee. He launched a kick that caught the man in the jaw, snapping his head back, and his jaw closed so hard that he bit through his tongue.

He turned on the first man then, and the man had

his gun in his hand. It was obvious from the way he trained it on Maddux that he had managed to reload.

"Shit!" Maddux said.

Joe Hannibal charged into the lobby, assessed the situation quickly, and reacted the only way he could.

He shot the man with the gun.

Maddux watched the man fall and breathed a sigh of relief. Only three years into his retirement he'd almost bought the farm, after cheating death for years.

Jesus, he thought, it makes a man think, don't it?

Three

Several people were injured, including Sue.

Maddux had rushed back into the dining room to see who was hurt, hoping that no one had been killed, and found Sue sitting on the ground, bleeding from a scratch on her left arm. She had her hand closed over it as he lifted her to her feet.

"Are you all right?" he asked, anxiously.

"I'm fine," she said, her eyes shining as she stared at him. "You were wonderful."

He hugged her to him then, not even thinking of what consequences might result from the move.

Later he and Hannibal went over to the doctor's office to check on the second man.

"We'd like to talk to him, Doc," Hannibal said.

The doctor's name was Algis Cleaver, but everyone called him Doc. He was in his sixties and had seen it all. Nothing surprised him anymore, not even a man with a near-bit-off tongue.

"Can't," Doc said.

"Why not?" Hannibal asked.

"He's got a pretty bad neck injury, and he bit

through his tongue so bad he might lose it, *and* his jaw's broke. You *could* talk to him, but he can't answer you."

"Shit!" Maddux said.

"Easy," Hannibal said. "Can he write his answers down?"

"Nope."

"Why not?" Hannibal asked. "Is his hand injured?"

"Nope."

"Then what is it?"

"First thing I asked him was could he write down his answers to my questions," Doc said. "Your man don't know how to write."

"Shit!" Hannibal said.

"Easy," Maddux said, mimicking Hannibal.

"Let's go to my office, Kyle," Hannibal said. "Keep me informed on his condition, huh, Doc?"

"Sure, Marshal, sure." Doc looked at Maddux and said, "What did you do to him?"

"I kicked him."

"You near killed him."

"I was trying to," Maddux said, and followed Hannibal out.

"Did you know him?" Hannibal asked in his office.

They both had a glass of whiskey, and the bottle was on the desk. Maddux's hands were shaking now that the danger was over, and his back was aching from lifting the table off the floor. But he also felt something else.

He felt exhilarated! He had never felt more alive in the past three years than in that dining room a little while before.

"Kyle?"

"What? I'm sorry."

"Did you know them?"

"No," Maddux said, frowning.

"Neither of them?"

"No."

"Then it can't be that they recognized you and felt they owed you, can it?"

"Sure it can," Maddux said. "Just because I don't know them doesn't mean they didn't know me. I've arrested a lot of people over the years, Joe, here and before I came to Cromwell. After thirty years of toting a badge, I can't be expected to remember all of them."

"Jesus, you're a talkative cuss tonight, ain't you?"

Maddux looked at Hannibal and said, "I'm sorry, Joe. I'm just a bit shook up, is all."

"Why? You been shot at with bad intentions before, ain't you?"

"Not in the last three years I ain't," Maddux said. He held up his whiskey glass so Hannibal could see that his hand was shaking, and then drained it. Hannibal emulated him, and then picked up the bottle and filled both glasses again.

"Kyle . . ." Hannibal said.

"Yeah, I know."

"Those fellas could have been hired to kill you."

"That's a possibility," Maddux said. "They did walk into the place, spot me, and open fire right away."

"Why?"

Maddux shrugged. "Like I said, a lot of people could have a lot of reasons for wanting me dead."

"I was hoping we could find out for sure from the other one."

"It don't look like we're gonna find out anything from him, not for a while anyway," Maddux said.

31

"I guess not."

"You could of took it easier on him."

"No, I couldn't," Maddux said. "Not in that situation. There were too many people around."

"Well, luckily no one was killed. The worst hurt was Bill Fowler. The rest was just scratched, scared, or got trampled."

"That doesn't make me feel any better."

"Hey, it wasn't your fault."

"Sure."

"It wasn't," Hannibal insisted. "Two hardcases come in and start blasting at you, how could you know that was gonna happen?"

"I could have figured it would happen sometime or another."

"Okay, and then what would you do?"

"Stay on my ranch."

"And do what? Send Joe Shadoweyes in for your supplies: He's a *real* welcome sight around these parts."

"All right, all right," Maddux said. He drained his glass and put it on the desk, waving off another drink. "I'm going to check on Sue."

"That gal's sweet on you, Maddux," Hannibal said. "You know that, don't you?"

"That's just plain sill—"

"And now you're her hero."

"Her hero," Maddux repeated bitterly. "I almost got her killed."

"Maddux—"

"Yeah, I know, not my fault," Maddux said, heading for the door. When he reached it, he turned and said, "Hey, Joe."

"Yeah?"

"Did I thank you for saving my life?"

"Not yet."

"Oh," Maddux said, "well, remind me to do it sometime, okay?"

"Gotcha."

"Good night."

"Night, Kyle."

Maddux went outside, and for a moment he felt some panic. What if there were others in town, men brought in to back up the first two shooters? What if they were drawing a bead on him right now?

Jesus, he told himself, you're seeing ghosts and goblins where there ain't any.

Nevertheless, as he walked down the street his aching back was stiff and erect and felt as if it had a target painted on it.

When Maddux got back home he told John Shadoweyes what had happened.

"That mare is gonna foal soon," Shadoweyes said. "I will keep an eye on her tonight."

"Did you hear what I said?" Maddux asked.

"Yes," Shadoweyes said, "you had some excitement in town."

"Two men tried to kill me, John," Maddux said. "If they were hired, then there'll be more on the way."

"So?"

"So maybe you better hightail it."

Shadoweyes gave Maddux a baleful stare and asked, "To where? This is the only home I have."

Shadoweyes had been working for Maddux for six months, and was worth his weight in gold. It was hard for Maddux to gauge his age. He could have been forty, or sixty. His long black hair had some gray in it, and he stood ramrod straight at about six-two. He was thin, but not as thin as when Maddux had hired him. Shadoweyes had been eating pretty good since he started working for Maddux. Maddux was glad to hear that he thought of the K & L Ranch as his home. Maybe he would stay off whiskey for good, but in this situation . . .

"John, you may be buying into trouble that's not yours," Maddux said.

"If anyone comes here looking for trouble," Shadoweyes said, "they are looking for me too."

"Is that your final word?" Maddux asked.

"It is."

"Well then," Maddux said, "we'd better get to work."

Shadoweyes nodded, and Maddux turned to go into the house. He had to break the news to Laura, and he decided to do so without repeating any of the conjecture he and Hannibal had gone through.

It was bad enough he had to tell her someone had tried to kill him, let alone that they might have been hired to do so.

Four

Over the next few days Maddux was tempted several times to go into town, but the incident was still fresh in his mind. Marshal Hannibal had said that as soon as the injured man could talk he'd question him, and if he found something out he'd come out to the ranch, but Hannibal had not shown up yet either. He also knew that if he decided to go to town it would precipitate an argument with Laura. She had not taken the news of the shooting well.

"Look at you," she'd shouted at him after he'd told her. "You haven't been this fired up in a long time. You liked it, didn't you?"

She had run into the bedroom and slammed the door before he could answer her.

He hadn't *liked* it—not exactly.

"Why don't you go into town?" Shadoweyes asked when he found Maddux standing on the porch, staring at the main road.

"And have somebody else get shot because of me?"

"That kind of talk is useless."

Maddux looked at Shadoweyes and said, "Yeah, I know it is. And we've still got some horses to break, and that mare has to foal—"

"She did," Shadoweyes said. "Last night."

"You didn't tell me."

Shadoweyes shrugged. "You have other things on your mind."

"How are they doing?"

"Mother and son are both fine."

"A colt, huh?" Maddux said. Thinking about the Arabian stallion the mare had been bred to, he said, "He's going to be a beauty."

"He already is," Shadoweyes said.

"Yeah," Maddux said. He tore his eyes away from the main road and said, "Come on, let's have a look at him."

Later that night, after Laura was asleep, Maddux took out what he had come to think of as his Backshooter map. He had traced the path of the Backshooter, from his first victim to his eleventh. Now he took his red marker and wrote in the twelfth victim.

It would be a long ride dogging the Backshooter's trail from victim one to victim twelve, but that would be the only way to find out who he was. Given the two-year period over which his twelve victims had been claimed, the man must have spent a reasonable amount of time in each area, establishing himself under one name or another. Somebody had to remember him. All Maddux would have to do was start matching names and descriptions. Pretty soon he'd know what to start looking for, even if he didn't know who.

That is, if he was going.

All the law knew was that people were being killed, shot in the back. The lawmen of each town were going no further than their own territory.

Maddux wondered why a federal marshal hadn't been sent to trail the Backshooter. Maybe the federal government didn't see this killing spree as a problem. Maybe that was because nobody important—like a banker, or a politician—had been killed yet. First time one of *them* bought the farm, you'd see how quick a federal marshal was on the scene.

Maybe that was why the Backshooter *hadn't* shot anyone important . . . yet.

Maddux folded the map and poured himself a cup of coffee from the bottom of the pot. He had the itch, all right, that was for sure. The question—if he was on the verge of making a decision—was whether or not he had the physical stamina for the job.

Laura would say no, but that was because she loved him and wouldn't want him to go.

If she loved him enough, though, maybe she *wouldn't* say no.

And maybe he'd go no matter what she thought.

A hell of a lot of maybes.

The next afternoon Shadoweyes came walking in from the barn and said, "Visitors coming."

"It's probably the marshal," Maddux said. "Maybe he got some information out of that fella."

"More than one rider," Shadoweyes said.

"I can't see anything yet."

"I can."

"The first rider?"

"A big, bulky man."

"Hannibal."

"Yes."

"And the second?"

"Not so big and bulky."

"Have Mrs. Maddux put up a pot of coffee, John."

Shadoweyes went inside, and Maddux watched until finally he too recognized Hannibal. He didn't know who the other man was.

He waited on the porch until both men reached the house and dismounted.

"Kyle," Hannibal said, by way of greeting.

"Afternoon, Joe," Maddux said. "You got any information for me?"

"Sorry, but Doc don't think that fella's ever gonna talk right. The swelling hasn't gone down on his tongue, yet, and he doesn't know how to write."

"Maybe I'll come on into town and ask him some yes-or-no questions. He could shake or nod his head."

"Could be," Hannibal said. "You're welcome to try it."

"Who's your friend?"

"Oh, sorry," Hannibal said. "This here is Mr. Glenn Wilkes, Kyle. Mr. Wilkes, this is Kyle Maddux."

The two men sized one another up.

Wilkes had the look of a dandy. Even his trail clothes were expensive, although they were covered with the same dust that Hannibal's clothes were. He was tall and slender, and Maddux noticed that he had soft hands. He wore a gun, but Maddux doubted that he knew how to use it."

"Mr. Wilkes," Maddux said. He moved to the edge of the porch and shook hands with the man. The handshake was firm enough.

"Mr. Maddux."

"Kyle, Mr. Wilkes came into Cromwell looking for you," Hannibal said.

"Really? We haven't met before, have we, Mr. Wilkes?" The question was a polite one. If Maddux had met this man before, he'd remember it.

38

"No, we haven't, Mr. Maddux," Wilkes said, "but I've heard all about you."

"Is that a fact?"

Hannibal, sensing that the meeting was not going well, said, "Can we take this inside, Kyle?"

"Sure, Joe. I've got coffee on—real coffee, not that piss you drink."

Maddux checked Wilkes to see if his language shocked the man, but his face never changed.

"Just tie your horses off. Shadoweyes will take care of them."

"Shadoweyes?" Wilkes said, frowning, looking at Hannibal.

"John Shadoweyes," Hannibal said. "He works for Maddux."

"With," Maddux said. "He works *with* me."

"With," Hannibal said. "Sorry."

Maddux moved into the house, followed by Hannibal and Wilkes.

Maddux sat in an old stuffed chair that he had gotten from the hotel when they were going to toss it out.

"Have a seat," he said to the other two men.

Laura came into the room and all three men stood up again. Maddux could see the look of admiration on Wilkes's face.

"Hello, Laura," Hannibal said.

"Marshal."

"Mr. Wilkes," Maddux said, "this is my wife, Laura."

"Mrs. Maddux," Wilkes said, "a pleasure."

Maddux noticed that Laura was dressed to go out.

"Kyle, I'm going to see Mrs. Hodges. She's ailing and could use some help around the house."

"All right," Maddux said.

He saw the look she gave both Hannibal and

Wilkes. She knew something was up, but she didn't want to hear about it now. She'd wait until she heard it from Maddux, later.

"Johh," Maddux said to Shadoweyes, "hitch up the buggy for Mrs. Maddux."

"Right."

That was the first time either Hannibal or Wilkes noticed Shadoweyes was in the room.

"Hello, John," Hannibal said.

"Marshal."

Shadoweyes went out, followed by Laura Maddux.

"You staying dinner, Joe?" Maddux asked.

"Who's cookin?" Hannibal asked, since it was obvious Laura wasn't going to be there.

Maddux laughed and said, "Shadoweyes."

"Then we'll stay."

Wilkes didn't seem to mind not being consulted.

Maddux brought three cups and the coffeepot to the table and sat down with them.

"Why don't you tell me what this is all about, Joe?" he asked.

Hannibal looked at Wilkes, who shrugged, indicating he didn't care who did the talking.

"Mr. Wilkes came to Cromwell looking for help, Maddux."

"Mine, or yours?"

"Yours."

"What seems to be his problem?"

"He's a Pinkerton agent."

"Is that a fact?"

"Maybe I should speak for myself," Wilkes said at this point. He looked at Maddux and said, "I'm after this fella some of the newspapers are calling the Backshooter."

"I've read about it," Maddux said. "What's Pinkerton's interest?"

40

"We've been hired by the family of one of the victims."

Maddux raised his eyebrows in surprise. "One of the victim's families is rich enough to afford Pinkerton?"

"I suppose so," Wilkes said. "I couldn't even tell you which family it was. All I know is that I've been assigned to track him down."

"And why are you here?"

"To ask you for your help."

"Why me?"

"Frankly," Wilkes said, "I didn't know who you were until Alan Pinkerton told me."

"Pinkerton and I are acquainted," Maddux said. Actually, he and Pinkerton knew each other very well. They didn't necessarily *like* each other, but they had respected each other over the years, and still did.

"What did he tell you?"

"He told me that since the Backshooter's trail started near here, in Abilene, that you were probably following the progress in the newspapers."

"Did he say why I might be doing that?"

"Yes," Wilkes said. "He said that in retirement you would have little else to do."

Damn him, Maddux thought.

"What do you want from me?" Maddux asked. "Advice?"

"No, sir," Wilkes said, "I want you to come with me."

Maddux stared at the man for a few moments, then looked at Hannibal, who just shrugged.

"Why?" Maddux asked.

"Frankly? I'm a city boy, Mr. Maddux. I need someone who can track him."

"Track him?" Maddux said. "How do you expect to follow a two-year-old trail?"

Wilkes cleared his throat. "Mr. Pinkerton said that no one can follow a cold trail like Kyle Maddux."

"Mr. Pinkerton is being very kind," Maddux said, sarcastically.

"Will you come?"

Maddux opened his mouth to say no, and then closed it. "Let's discuss it again after dinner," he said.

Five

After dinner Hannibal joined Maddux out on the porch. Inside, Wilkes was having a cup of coffee, being watched closely by John Shadoweyes.

"Give it all to me, Joe," Maddux said.

They hadn't discussed it over dinner because Maddux needed some time to digest the information that had been sprung on him.

"All I know is what the man told me, Maddux," Hannibal said. "He came to my office, introduced himself, and told me he was a Pinkerton agent and he was looking for you."

"Did he tell you why?"

"I wouldn't bring him out here until he did."

"What else did he tell you?"

"He thinks the Backshooter is more than one man."

"What makes him say that?"

Hannibal hesitated, "He thinks some of the Backshooter's killings were done by Walker Bogart."

"Walker—" Maddux started, looking at Hannibal. He paused a moment, then said, "Well, now this makes a little more sense."

Walker Bogart's name had started hitting the

papers just about the time Maddux had retired—and about the same time as the Backshooter. During the past year his legend had been growing, to the point where his name was being mentioned in the same breath with the great ones—the James boys, Billy the Kid, and Clay Allison as an outlaw, and Hickok as a gunman.

"This Wilkes is after the reward on Bogart," said Maddux, "and he's disguising his hunt with this Backshooter business."

"Why would he do that?" Hannibal asked. "Why not just go after Bogart?"

"Maybe this was the only way he could get Pinkerton to foot his bills."

"Wait a minute," Hannibal said, suddenly excited. "This might be making more sense than we know."

"How do you mean?"

"What if Bogart heard that you might be coming after him?"

"How would he hear that?"

"Never mind how," Hannibal said. "What if he did? What would he do?"

Maddux knew what Hannibal was getting at. "Maybe he'd send some hired guns to kill me."

"Right."

"Well," Maddux said, "we'll have to ask the one we have in town."

Hannibal agreed.

"What's the price up to now?"

"Bogart?"

Maddux nodded.

"Five thousand. He's murdered seven people, among his other crimes."

Maddux rubbed his hand over his face. "Nineteen between him and this other crazy man."

"What if we took Wilkes's theory a step further?"

44

Hannibal asked.

"How?"

"What if he and the Backshooter are the same person?"

"And what if there's no connection at all?"

"If Wilkes's theory is right, and it's not just a dodge, then there's a possibility that when we find Bogart we'll find the Backshooter. If not, then we'll just find Bogart, and maybe along the way you'll get a clue about who the Backshooter is."

Maddux turned and stared at Hannibal. He had noticed that Hannibal was saying "we" a lot."

"You're the marshal of Cromwell, Joe. You can't go off hunting a deadly killer because of another man's theory."

"I could, if a friend asked me."

"Meaning me?"

"You are gonna go, aren't you?"

"For him?" Maddux asked, jerking his head in the direction of the house.

"For him, for your friend Pinkerton . . . for yourself."

Rubbing his mouth with his hand, Maddux said, "I thought I had my last hunt, Joe."

"Three years ago."

"Yeah," Maddux said, thinking back. "That was a bad one, you know?"

"I know," Hannibal said, "I'm the one who found you, remember?"

"That one made me realize that after thirty years of hunting men for a living—among my other duties— the odds were definitely not in my favor anymore."

"What odds . . . for what?"

"Survival."

"You mean that even if you hadn't been shot in the back you might have retired?"

"It's possible."

Maddux looked straight out over his land, and Hannibal gave him a moment with his thoughts. Hannibal doubted that Maddux would have retired if his back hadn't forced him into it. Kyle Maddux had enjoyed the work too much, even after thirty years. It was the back injury—and Laura, of course—that had forced him into it.

Now he was going to have to defy both.

"There's a catch to this," Hannibal said, breaking the silence, "if you do agree to go."

"What catch?"

"Don't forget that Wilkes will be going along."

Maddux snorted derisively. "He'd get his clothes all dirty!"

"I guess that don't matter to him much," Hannibal said. "If he finds Bogart he gets the reward. If he finds the Backshooter, Pinkerton will reward him. Either way he can't lose, can he?"

"Only we can," Maddux said, "if he gets us killed."

Maddux took a moment to think, leaning against a post with his right thumb hooked into his back pocket. "Well, I've got a catch of my own then."

"What's that?"

"Shadoweyes comes."

"Shadoweyes?"

"He's a damned good tracker."

"When he's sober."

"I told you—"

"I know what you told me," Hannibal said.

"You can stay behind, Joe," Maddux said. "No point risking your job—"

"My job'll be there when I get back," Hannibal said. "Besides, who else would want to be the marshal of a town called Cromwell?"

"You've got a point there."

"Well?"

"Well what?"

"Are we going?"

Maddux made a face. "Let's go in and see if we can't talk the damn fool out of coming with us and slowing us down."

"And do his work for him?"

"If we're going to go, Joe," Maddux said, "what do we need him for?"

Hannibal smiled.

"Don't forget who'll be footing the bill," Hannibal said. "I know enough about you and Pinkerton to know that you won't mind taking advantage of *that*."

As it turned out, Glenn Wilkes was adamant about Shadoweyes not going. He had an Easterner's distrust of Indians.

"There's really no *good* reason for the Ind—uh, for Mr. Shadoweyes to come, is there?"

"There is," Maddux said.

"And what would that be?"

"Because he can track a mountain cat through a stone canyon."

"I'm . . . not sure I know what that means."

"It means he's an expert tracker, Mr. Wilkes," Hannibal said.

"That's what I said," Maddux said.

"I see," Wilkes said. He looked at Maddux and said, "I thought you were the expert tracker."

"Four eyes are better than two," Maddux said.

"And you, Marshal?" Wilkes asked. "Do you vouch for Shadoweyes?"

All eyes were on Hannibal now, waiting for his

answer. To his credit he gave it with only the slightest hint of hesitation. "He's a good man, Mr. Wilkes."

"Well, all right," Wilkes said, "but I will not pay him. That will be up to you, Mr. Maddux."

"If he'll come at all, Mr. Wilkes," Maddux said, "you'll pay him, or I won't come."

Shadoweyes sat in a corner of the room and didn't say anything. Maddux knew he'd come, and that was all that mattered.

"Well," Wilkes said, grudgingly, "all right, Marshal, can we get back to town now? I have some wires to send."

"Sure, Mr. Wilkes," Hannibal said.

"Joe," Maddux said, "Shadoweyes and I will be along at first light. We'll want to talk to Doc's patient first."

"Patient?" Wilkes said.

"Another matter, Wilkes," Hannibal said.

"Mr. Maddux, I'll expect your full attention to *this* matter," Wilkes said pompously.

"You'll get it, Wilkes," Maddux said. "My undivided attention."

"We have not settled on a fee—" Wilkes started.

"I'm sure you'll pay me fairly, Mr. Wilkes," Maddux said, "with Mr. Pinkerton's money."

Glenn Wilkes looked puzzled at Maddux's attitude when it came to the money. It was probably an attitude he had never encountered before in the East.

"I'll walk you gentlemen out."

When Maddux went back inside, John Shadoweyes had the place cleaned up and a fresh pot of coffee on the stove.

"Cup?" Shadoweyes asked.

48

"Sure."

Maddux sat down at the table and Shadoweyes set a cup of coffee in front of him.

"Are we going?" Shadoweyes asked.

"I'm going," Maddux said, sipping the coffee. Shadoweyes made the best coffee he'd ever tasted, and the Indian refused to tell him what he put in it.

"Whether or not you're going is up to you," Maddux said, putting his cup back down. "You hired on to break horses and help me run the ranch, not hunt men."

"If you are going, Maddux," Shadoweyes said, "I am going."

Maddux looked at John Shadoweyes and then decided not to ask why.

The answer might embarrass both of them.

"What are you going to tell Mrs. Maddux?" Shadoweyes asked.

Maddux looked at the other man and said, "I've been wondering the same thing myself."

Six

In the morning Maddux and Shadoweyes closed up the house. Laura, incensed that Maddux had decided to go, said that she would be staying with Mrs. Hodges until Maddux returned.

She also hinted that she might not be ready to come back when Maddux returned. "But we can talk about that, Kyle. Go and get this out of your system, and we'll talk about it *if* you come back."

On the way to town they stopped off at their nearest neighbor's and asked Tom Seals if he'd come over and pick up the horses that were in the corral. Maddux trusted Seals to complete his transaction with the Army. It was one of the things that made this life so different from his other life—trusting people.

He was preparing to move back into the old life, though, and evidence of that was the gun on his hip and the anticipatory emptiness in the pit of his stomach. He did not feel particularly comfortable with either one of them at the moment.

After leaving Tom Seal's place they rode directly to Cromwell and stopped in front of Marshal Joe Hannibal's office. Inside Hannibal was talking to his two deputies, Ed Gorman and Al Collins.

Gorman was the older of the two and would be the man put in charge until Hannibal returned. He was in his mid-forties, and this particular star was just one of many he'd worn over the years. His scarred face and hands were evidence of the fact that there were times he upheld the law without the use of a gun.

Al Collins was in his thirties, and yet he could have passed for a youth in his early twenties. He was one of those men who always look ten years younger than they were. Of course, when he was seventy, that wouldn't matter much.

"Come on in, Maddux," Hannibal said. Shadow-eyes had remained outside with the horses. Maddux knew that the man had no desire to step inside the marshal's office.

"All right," Hannibal said to the deputies, "you boys know what to do."

Gorman and Collins nodded, greeted Maddux, and wished him luck on their way out.

"Have you talked to the town fathers?" Maddux asked.

"Yesterday evening, after Wilkes and I got back," Hannibal said. "They didn't like it, but then they don't have to."

"Joe, tell me your read on Wilkes."

"Self-important," Hannibal said, ticking points off his fingers, "a real pain in the ass—"

"Come on, Marshal," Maddux said, "don't hold back. Tell me what you really think."

Hannibal scowled at Maddux's humor, but was unable to hold it for very long.

"Where's Shadoweyes?" Hannibal asked after the laughter had subsided.

"Outside with the horses. Have you arranged for supplies?"

Hannibal nodded and said, "There'll be a pack horse waiting at the livery. Uh, Susan would like to see you before you leave."

Maddux stared at Hannibal and said, "How did she find out I was leaving?"

"Well, uh . . ." Hannibal stammered, looking sheepish.

"You told her, didn't you?"

"It slipped out last night, while she was serving me dinner."

"Shit."

"She's working this morning."

Maddux shifted his feet and said, "Yeah, all right, I'll go and see her."

"That's a right nice gal, Maddux," Hannibal said. "You could do a lot worse—"

"Believe me, I've got enough problems with one woman, Joe," Maddux said, holding both hands up to stop his friend from going any further. He told the lawman Laura Maddux's feelings about the trip.

"Doesn't sound like you got much of a send-off," Hannibal said, commiserating.

"I didn't."

"Well, maybe Susan can—"

"I'll meet you at the livery. Can I trust you with Shadoweyes? I mean, you won't arrest him or anything?"

"What for?"

"I don't know," Maddux said, shrugging. "You're just ornery enough to think of something."

"I ain't ornery—" Hannibal was saying as Maddux went out the door.

"John, I have to go over to the hotel," Maddux said

to Shadoweyes outside. "Why don't you take the horses to the livery. There should be a pack horse waiting. Check it out, okay?"

"Yes."

"I'll meet you and the marshal and Wilkes there."

The Indian scowled, and walked into the office without another word.

Seven

As luck would have it Glenn Wilkes was seated at the table Susan was serving when Maddux entered. She saw Maddux and motioned him over. Reluctantly, Maddux approached the table.

Wilkes had been speaking, placing his order, and had not seen Susan wave Maddux over. When he looked up and saw Maddux, he assumed that Maddux was coming to see him.

"Maddux," he said, his tone scolding, "I don't make a habit of discussing business at breakfast."

"Well that's good, Wilkes," Maddux said, "because I'm not here to see you." He looked at Susan and asked, "Do you have his order?"

"Yes."

"Well, let's go put it in."

He took her arm, careful of her injury, and led her to the kitchen. Before talking to him, she gave Wilkes's order to the cook.

"I understand Hannibal told you we were leaving."

"Yes," she said. "I wanted to see you before you left. I want to . . . to . . ."

She was faltering and he decided to let her work it

out on her own. "I wanted to tell you to be careful."

"Did he tell you where we were going?"

"No."

"Or why?"

"No."

"Then why do you feel the need to tell me to be careful?"

"Well, he's leaving with you. The marshal wouldn't do that unless whatever you were doing was important—or dangerous."

"Susan . . ."

She smiled at him and touched his mouth with her hand. He was as startled as if she had kissed him, and looked appropriately guilty.

"I won't embarrass you," she said, "I just wanted to say good-bye, and to ask you to be sure to come back."

"I have every intention of doing that."

"Fine," she said, and went back to work.

Maddux stepped out of the kitchen and saw Wilkes standing outside waiting for him.

"Saying good-bye to your lady friend?" Maddux did not like the look on Wilkes's face, as if the two of them now shared a secret of some sort.

"Saying good-bye to a friend," Maddux said. "What's it to you?"

"I'm just not used to being ignored by my employees, in favor of a waitress," Wilkes said, "although I must admit she's very—"

He stopped short when Maddux's forefinger poked him hard in the chest. "Let's get something straight here, Wilkes," he said, pressing hard with his finger. "I am not your employee. I work for myself."

"I understood that—"

"You understood wrong."

Rubbing his chest where he'd been poked, Wilkes

said, "You're taking my money."

"I haven't taken a cent yet," Maddux reminded him, "and it remains to be seen if I will—and *if* I do, it will be Alan Pinkerton's money, not yours. Now, we're ready to leave. Are you coming?"

"I've just ordered breakfast."

"Fine," Maddux said, "you stay and have your breakfast."

Maddux headed for the lobby, unaware that Susan was watching his progress.

"Now, hold on," Glenn Wilkes called out, following him.

Maddux turned on Wilkes in the lobby.

"The marshal, Shadoweyes, and I will be at the livery stable for the next fifteen minutes," he said. "If you're coming, you'll be there by then."

He turned and left the hotel without giving the man a chance to reply.

If it hadn't been so early, and the street so empty, Maddux might have died right there and then. As it was, Maddux detected a slight movement from the corner of his eye as he left the hotel and threw himself into the street. If nothing had happened he would have looked pretty silly—but it was better than being dead.

The man he had seen began firing the exact second Maddux dove from the boardwalk. As Maddux landed he pulled his gun, came around on his knees, and fired twice at the man. The first shot caught the man right in the belly, the second in the heart, killing him instantly.

People came running out of the hotel, and Marshal Hannibal came from his office.

"Jesus," Hannibal said, "another one?"

"Somebody wants me dead pretty bad, Joe," Maddux said, reloading his weapon, his eyes sweeping the street for further danger.

"Could be Bogart."

"Could be anyone," Maddux said. "It's not going to be so safe to be riding with me."

"Safe is just another word for boring," Hannibal said, "and I hate being bored."

"All right," Maddux said, snapping the gun shut. "Maybe you'd better get someone to clean up here and then meet me at the doctor's."

"I won't be long," Hannibal said.

Maddux started for the livery, wondering if someone was stepping out of his past with these two attempts on his life, or if it really was Walker Bogart. If it was the latter, then the man feared him for some reason.

Or maybe he was just sending him a calling card.

Eight

Maddux had to wake the doctor and apologized for it.

"Don't apologize," the doctor said. "Usually people wake me up because somebody's hurt or dead. I prefer your reasons."

"Can I talk to him?"

"I imagine he's asleep," the doctor said, "but I don't think that will stop you, eh?"

"No, it won't."

"He can't talk very well," the older man said. "He's developed an infection and I'm afraid I'm going to have to take his tongue."

"The man tried to kill me, doc," Maddux said. "The last thing I'd feel for him is pity."

"Go on in, then," the doctor said, scratching at his head of gray hair.

Maddux entered the room where the injured man lay sleeping. He walked over to the bed and slapped the man in the forehead.

"Uh—" the man said, coming awake. His eyes, fuzzy with sleep, cleared when he saw Maddux.

They cleared even more when Maddux put the barrel of the gun up against his jaw.

"I'm going to ask you some questions," Maddux said. "They are yes-or-no questions. You answer with a nod for yes, or a shake of the head for no. Do you understand me?"

The man's eyes, wide with fright, fastened on Maddux's face as he nodded.

"Were you sent to kill me by Walker Bogart?"

The man closed his eyes. He started to lick his lips, and then hissed at the pain the move caused.

"If you're worried about Bogart killing you," Maddux said, pressing the gun tightly against the man's chin, "you better worry some about me. I'll ask you again. Were you sent by Walker Bogart?"

The man opened his eyes, looked into Maddux's eyes, and was moved by what he saw there to nod his head.

"Well, that's good," Maddux said. "That's real good." Now he didn't have to rack his brain trying to figure out who was rising up out of his past.

"Do you know where Bogart is now?"

A shake of the head indicated no.

"Did you get paid in advance?"

A nod, for yes.

"How many of you—did he send two of you?"

The man shook his head no.

"Three?"

A nod.

"And you decided that one of you would lay back, in case the first two failed?"

Another nod.

"All right," Maddux said. He cocked the hammer back on the gun and the man began to whimper. When the man closed his eyes, Maddux took the gun away from his face and brought the hammer back down.

"Think of me when the doctor cuts off your

60

tongue, and don't be here when I get back."

The man remained with his eyes closed, his face drenched with sweat, as Maddux left the room.

"And you believed him?" Hannibal said back at the livery.

"Yes," Maddux said. "He wasn't in a position where he could afford to lie."

"I won't ask what that means."

"Have you got paper on Bogart?"

"I was waiting for you to ask," Hannibal said. He took a folded poster from his back pocket and handed it over.

Maddux opened it up and looked at it. As usual, the drawing of a man's face could have been anyone. The physical description said Bogart was six-four, with sandy-colored hair and a scar on the right side of his neck.

"Bogart is supposed to be good with a gun," Maddux said.

"Very good."

"That's odd for a big man," Maddux said, thoughtfully. "Can I keep this?"

"Sure."

Maddux refolded it and put it in his back pocket.

"You've got a funny look on your face," Hannibal said.

"I do?"

"Yes, you do," Hannibal said. "You're feeling it again, aren't you?"

"Feeling what?"

"The thrill of the hunt."

"Could be," Maddux said. He realized that this was not a denial, but then he couldn't very well deny it. There had been a surge of something when

Hannibal handed him the poster, and it had nothing to do with the five-thousand-dollar reward.

John Shadoweyes was standing in the shadows, listening to the conversation, saying nothing.

"Where's Wilkes, I wonder?" Hannibal said then.

"If we're lucky he decided to have his breakfast," Maddux said. He looked at Shadoweyes and asked, "How is the pack horse?"

"The marshal picked him out."

That was the way Shadoweyes would say he hadn't checked the animal.

"I know horseflesh, Maddux," Hannibal said.

"If you picked him out, then I'm satisfied, Joe," Maddux said.

Maddux saw Hannibal looking over his shoulder, and turned to see Glenn Wilkes hurrying toward them.

"I'll saddle his horse," Hannibal said.

"Let him saddle his own damned horse!" Maddux said.

Hannibal just gave Maddux a look and went to saddle the horse.

Nine

Ceremony, New Mexico

Walker Bogart was enjoying his breakfast.

He was eating with the hearty gusto of a man who had no worries in the world.

In fact, as far as he was concerned, he *didn't* have any worries. He was eating in the dining room of the Ceremony House Hotel, and was far from finished when his man Jerry Parnell entered and approached his table.

"You ain't gonna tell me something that's gonna ruin my appetite, Jerry, are you?" he demanded before Parnell could speak.

"Uh, it ain't my fault, Walker," Jerry Parnell said, whining.

"Jesus," Bogart said, dropping his fork in disgust. "I can't eat when you whine like that. What the hell is the problem now?"

Parnell shifted his feet, then blurted out, "Maddux ain't dead."

Bogart stared at Parnell long enough for the man to start to fidget from foot to foot.

"And why ain't Maddux dead?" Bogart finally asked.

"Well—"

"How many men did you send to do the job?"

"Three to do the job, and one to report on it."

"And what happened to them?"

"Two of them are dead."

"And the third one?"

"He was hurt."

"How bad?"

"I—don't rightly know, Walker."

"So Maddux took all three of them?"

"Yep." Parnell shuffled his feet.

"And whose decision was it to send three men to do the job on him?"

"Uh, mine."

"And who was wrong?"

"I was."

"Remember that, Jerry," Bogart said.

"Remember what, Walker?"

"That I'm always right and you're always wrong."

"Aw, Walker—"

"Shut up," Bogart said. He was a big man, broad across the shoulders and chest, and even seated he seemed to dwarf Jerry Parnell—but it wasn't the sheer size of Bogart that frightened Parnell. It was the fact that Parnell had personally seen Walker Bogart kill six men—two of them with his bare hands, and one of those just for spilling coffee on him.

"Shut up and get out of here," Bogart said. "Find out about that third man, and whether or not he's gonna talk to the law."

"Right."

"I want to know if Maddux's coming after me."

"I'll find out."

Parnell didn't move. Bogart picked up his fork,

saw that Parnell was there, and then put it down again. He fixed the man with an impatient stare.

"Now what?" Bogart asked.

"What about the girl?"

"What about her?"

"What do we do with her?"

"You do what I said to do."

"Uh, why don't we just kill her, Walker?"

Bogart assumed an expression not unlike that worn by a schoolteacher addressing a slow-witted child.

"I told you, Jerry, she's just too damned pretty to kill."

"She's dangerous, Walker."

"*She* ain't so dangerous where she is now, is she?" Bogart asked.

"No, but—"

"Jerry, I'm gonna be known not only as the man who brought Maddux out of retirement, but as the man who killed him as well. Do you understand that?"

Parnell didn't. If Bogart wanted to kill Maddux himself, then why did he have Parnell send the men to Cromwell to bushwhack him?

"I still think she's dangerous on her own—" Parnell began.

"Jerry?"

"What?"

"Who's always right?"

Looking sheepish Parnell said, "You are."

"And who's always wrong?"

In a low voice the other man said, "I am."

"Get out!"

"Right, Walker."

"Jerry!"

Parnell, already a few steps away, turned and came

back. "Yeah, Walker?"

Bogart beckoned to him and Parnell leaned over the table, very conscious of the fact that he was now within the big man's reach.

"I don't want her hurt or killed—"

"Sure, Walk—"

"—and I don't want her touched either. Do you know what I mean by *touched?*"

"Uh, sure, Walker, I know. You don't want her, uh . . . touched."

"Right. You'll pass that along to those two idiots you have watching her, won't you?"

"I sure will, Walker."

"Good," Bogart said. "Now you can get out."

The other diners in the room did not hear the conversation, but when they saw the smaller man hurriedly scurrying from the dining room they knew he was propelled by fear.

The big man looked down at his breakfast then and frowned. He called for the waiter loudly and told him that his food had gone cold.

"But sir," the waiter said, "it got cold while you were talking to you friend—"

"I don't care *why* it got cold," the big man said, frowning. "I just know that it is."

"I'll . . . have it reheated for you, sir."

"I don't want it reheated, man," Walker Bogart said, "I want it replaced." He held the plate aloft and said, "I want a fresh plate. I'm a guest of this hotel. Don't you take care of your guests?"

"Uh, yes, sir, we do."

"Well, then?"

The waiter smiled nervously and picked up the plate from the table. "I'll bring you a fresh plate, sir."

"Thank you very much."

As the waiter headed for the kitchen another diner

called out to him.

"Yes, sir?" the waiter said, holding the big man's plate away from him.

"Waiter," the man said, rather timidly because he wasn't sure if this was going to work or not, *"my breakfast seems to have gotten cold."*

The waiter frowned at the man and barked, "Eat it anyway."

Ten

They rode into New Moon, Texas, sixteen days after leaving Cromwell. They had stopped first in Abilene, where the Backshooter had claimed his first victim. The second victim had been killed in New Moon.

"Small town," Hannibal commented.

"Big enough to have a telegraph office," Maddux said, pointing to it.

"What are we going to do here?" Glenn Wilkes asked impatiently.

The man had asked a lot of questions all along the way. Things like "Why can't I drink more water?" and "How do you expect me to eat that?" and "Are you sure we're going the right way?"

Maddux looked at Wilkes and said with as much patience as he could muster, "Right now we're going to have the horses taken care of, and then get us a couple of hotel rooms."

"A couple of rooms? Don't we need four?"

"Two will be plenty."

Wilkes look appalled.

"Don't worry, Mr. Wilkes," Maddux said. "You can bunk in with the marshal."

That didn't seem to appease the man any. In the end Wilkes offered to pay for three rooms so he could have his own.

"That's up to you," Maddux said. "John and I will share a room anyway, though."

So Marshal Joe Hannibal ended up with a room of his own.

When they got to the livery John Shadoweyes said, "I will see to the horses."

They all gave their mounts over to Shadoweyes and Maddux said, "Meet us at the nearest hotel."

"Right."

As Maddux, Hannibal, and Wilkes walked away from the livery to find the hotel Wilkes said, "Shouldn't we go to the telegraph office?"

"All in good time, Mr. Wilkes," Hannibal said. He replied because he knew that Maddux's patience with the man was just about at an end. "There are some other things we have to do first."

"Like what?"

"Like—" Hannibal began, but Maddux cut him off.

"Look!" he said, whirling on Wilkes. "We're going to get along a lot better with each other if you'd stop asking so damn many questions."

"I'm just concerned—"

"Being concerned is my job," Maddux said. "All *you* have to do is follow me. Understand?"

"Look, Kyle," Hannibal said, "why don't you go to the saloon and wait for us there. We'll take care of getting the rooms."

"I'm going to check in with the local law, Joe."

"Shouldn't I do that?" Hannibal asked. "After all, I'm a lawman—"

"Not on this trip you're not," Maddux said. "I'll check in with him and then meet you at the saloon, like you suggested."

"All right, Maddux," Hannibal said. "It's your show."

"Thank you," Maddux said, and walked away from them.

Maddux found the sheriff's office with no trouble and entered without knocking. He caught the man behind the desk in the act of pulling on one of his boots. It was a difficult act because the man's mountainous belly was getting in his way.

He finally slid the boot on and then slammed his foot onto the floor.

"Damn marriage!" the man said, and then noticed Maddux standing there.

"What has marriage to do with getting a boot on?"

"I'll tell you, stranger, so you can keep it in mind before *you* ever marry," the sheriff said. "Once I was as slender as you, and then I married a woman who could cook. Now I got this gut."

"I see."

The sheriff straightened behind his desk and said, "But you didn't come here to talk about my problems. What can I do for you, mister?"

"My name's Maddux, Sheriff. . . ."

"Oh, sorry," the lawman said. "Name's Kiley, Andy Kiley."

"Sheriff Kiley, my name is Kyle Maddux. I'm here in town with a Pinkerton agent."

"Really? I ain't never met a Pinkerton agent."

"I'll be sure to introduce you."

"That's right nice of you. Just what are you fellas doing in New Moon?"

"Sheriff, you had a murder here a couple of years ago."

"That?" the sheriff said.

"You know which one I'm talking about?"

71

"We ain't had that many murders in this county, Mr. Maddux. You're talking about old Pop Wingate bein' shot in the back by that fella they're callin' the Backshooter. Right?"

"That's the one," Maddux said.

"Why you here lookin' into that after all this time?"

"It's a long story, Sheriff," Maddux said. "Let's just say I'm dogging a cold trail."

"You sure are."

"I wanted you to know that we'd be talking to people in town about it, and probably the family as well."

"Only family Pop had was his daughter, Patricia, and she left after he was killed."

That didn't surprise Maddux. They had run into the same situation in Abilene. The man who had been killed there had been a young man, and his wife had left town soon after.

"That's all right," Maddux said. "We'll still be talking to the townspeople about it—that is, if you don't mind."

"Suit yourself," the sheriff said with a shrug. "That's all old business to me."

That was the attitude Maddux had expected to run into dealing with local law. He'd have been surprised by anything else.

"Well, thanks very much, Sheriff. I appreciate your time."

Maddux turned and started for the door.

"Maddux?"

Maddux turned and said, "Yes?"

"Uh, will you and your friends be staying in town long?"

"Just a few days, I think," Maddux said, his hand on the doorknob. "Long enough for my friends and

72

me to talk to most of the people who knew Pop Wingate."

"Well then, good luck," Kiley said. "And if you're interested in knowing, the Hotel of New Moon has a fine dining room."

As the man spoke he rubbed his belly, and Maddux knew he was speaking from experience.

"Thank you, Sheriff," Maddux said. "I'll keep that in mind."

Maddux left the office, and the sheriff sat back in his chair and assumed a worried look.

Eleven

Maddux walked into the saloon and found Hannibal and Wilkes at a table, sharing a bottle of whiskey. Actually, Hannibal was drinking the whiskey, and Wilkes was complaining that the saloon didn't have any brandy.

"It's a small town, Mr. Wilkes," Hannibal was saying as Maddux approached the table.

If Wilkes was going to reply, he was interrupted by Maddux's appearance.

"Kyle," Hannibal said, "take a chair."

Maddux sat down and Hannibal filled the glass he'd provided for him.

"Thanks," Maddux said, taking a taste.

"Did you find out anything from the sheriff?" Hannibal asked.

"Oh, he had some words of wisdom about marriage, and eating, and putting your boots on—"

"What?" Wilkes said.

"—but he had nothing to say about the murder, except that the dead man's daughter left town soon after. He didn't know anything about the murder."

"Did you believe him?" Wilkes said.

Maddux didn't answer right away.

"I have no reason not to believe him, Wilkes," he finally answered, wearily. He looked at Hannibal and asked, "Did you get the hotel rooms?"

"Yes," Hannibal said.

"Good. I'll see you back there. I figure we'll have dinner in the hotel dining room."

"That's fine," Hannibal said.

Maddux stood up and left the saloon, leaving his drink unfinished.

"Mr. Wilkes," Hannibal said, "you're gonna have to try and get along with Maddux."

"Why?" Wilkes asked. "I am employing him. *He* should be trying to get along with *me*. If he's not careful, I'll fire him."

"If you fire him you'll never find . . . what you're looking for."

"You mean you couldn't find Walker Bogart?" Wilkes asked with disdain. "Or the Backshooter?"

"Mr. Wilkes, I'm a good lawman, but when it comes to tracking there ain't a better man than Maddux."

"If he's so good, why did he retire?"

"Well, I guess that's something you're gonna have to ask him—but he sure won't answer that question while you and him are sniping at each other."

Hannibal picked up the bottle and poured himself and Wilkes another drink. It occurred to him that he had left Cromwell to play nursemaid to two men who were just as likely to kill each other as not.

Twelve

When Maddux left the saloon he decided to take a turn around town and try to talk to some of the people about Pop Wingate. It was something he had also done in Abilene, talking to people about Del Kilmer, the man who had been killed there.

In both cases people were fairly willing to talk about the two men, indicating that the victims were, for the most part, well-liked men. But when he started asking about people who might have been hanging around the two men, that's when people didn't have much to say.

Maddux was looking for someone who might have noticed a stranger who had come to town and become involved with the dead man. He was also looking for information on someone who might have left town right after the killing—other than family, that is.

As he had in Abilene, he came up empty in New Moon. The killings had simply happened too long ago for people to remember anything other than the people who were killed.

When Maddux got to the room he was sharing with Shadoweyes, he found the man sitting on the floor, even though there were two beds in the room.

"Bad mattresses?"

Shadoweyes looked at him and said, "They are almost like lying on the ground."

"But not as comfortable, huh?"

"No."

Maddux sat on one of the beds and discovered that Shadoweyes was right. He took a moment to sit there and close his eyes, trying to will away the pain in his back. Stretching would do no good—about as much good as willing the pain away did.

"Is it bad?" Shadoweyes asked.

Maddux looked over his shoulder at the man and said, "It's there."

"The riding—" Shadoweyes started to say, but Maddux cut him off.

"Hasn't made it any worse . . . yet," Maddux lied. He knew that his back *was* hurting more because of the riding, but then so was his backside. It had been a long time since he had done any serious riding. He was hoping that his back and butt would hurt less after a few more miles in the saddle.

"Bad news?" Shadoweyes asked. Maddux knew they were off the subject of his back and onto the subject of what he had found out.

"No news," Maddux said.

Briefly, he told Shadoweyes about his visit to the sheriff, his conversation with Wilkes, and then his talk with some of the townspeople about Pop Wingate.

"People will remember more when we get closer to Mexico," Shadoweyes said.

Maddux frowned. By the time they reached the site of the twelfth and most recent murder, it would be almost three months old—and there might be another one in the meantime.

"Maybe," he said. "I'm having dinner in the hotel dining room with Hannibal and . . . Wilkes. Do you want to come?"

"I do not think so," Shadoweyes said. "I do not think Mr. Wilkes and I should sit at the same table."

"Look, John," Maddux said, "if he doesn't like it, then he can go and sit somewhere else."

"No, I do not worry that he will not like it," Shadoweyes said. "I know *I* will not like it."

"All right then."

"I will find someplace else to eat, and keep my ears open."

"Okay, you do that," Maddux said. He walked to the window and looked down at New Moon's main street. "We'll meet up here later and see if either of us has come up with anything useful."

John Shadoweyes nodded and stood up.

"I wish you luck," Shadoweyes said. "I do not envy you having dinner with that man."

"I don't know what it is, John," Maddux said. "We've just taken an instant dislike to each other."

"That is easy to understand—on your part."

"Yeah, well, maybe I should just make more of an effort to be civil with him."

"I am glad the effort is yours to make," Shadoweyes said, "and not mine."

"Yeah," Maddux said as Shadoweyes went out the door.

At dinner Maddux decided that if he couldn't say anything civil to Wilkes, he wouldn't speak to the man at all.

"Where's Shadoweyes?" Hannibal asked.

"He's eating somewhere else."

"That's just as well," Glenn Wilkes said. "I don't relish having my meals with an Indian."

"Shadoweyes is a half-breed," Hannibal said, correcting him.

"That is even worse," Wilkes said. "There's *nothing* worse than someone whose blood isn't pure."

Maddux held his tongue.

"What's Shadoweyes really doing?" Hannibal asked.

"Keeping his eyes and ears open."

"Excuse me," Wilkes said, "but I'm not paying—"

"Shadoweyes works for me," Maddux said, forestalling any objections Wilkes might have.

"Very well," Wilkes said. His tone was imperious, as if he had just given his permission for something.

Maddux held his tongue.

"What are we going to do?" Hannibal asked.

"I'll talk to Shadoweyes in a few hours," Maddux said. "If he hasn't come up with anything, then I'll make another visit to the sheriff and see if I can't jar his memory a little."

"We'll be leaving tomorrow?" Hannibal asked.

"I think so," Maddux said. "There doesn't seem to be much reason to stay any longer."

"One day doesn't seem like very much effort," Wilkes said.

Maddux gave Wilkes a cold look. "Are you really a Pinkerton?" he asked.

The man looked surprised at the question.

"Of course I am."

"I never did see any of your papers."

Wilkes's chin seemed to stiffen as he fished his wallet out of his pocket and showed Maddux his certification that he was a Pinkerton agent.

"What do you want?" he asked Wilkes, passing the wallet back.

"What?"

"I asked you what you want? Why you're here?"

Wilkes looked at Hannibal, then said, "I want to find the Backshooter."

"Or Walker Bogart."

"Yes."

Maddux shook his head and said, "It doesn't figure."

"What doesn't?" Hannibal asked.

"Him being a Pink," Maddux said. "He hasn't done a lick of work either here or in Abilene.

"I beg your pardon," Wilkes said. "My methods happen to be subtle."

Maddux studied Wilkes, nodding his head to himself, and then said, "It just doesn't figure."

"And why not?" Wilkes asked, stiffly.

"You're not Alan Pinkerton's type," Maddux said. "Who hired you?"

"I was hired by William Pinkerton."

"Out of Chicago?" Maddux asked.

"Yes."

"And sent to the St. Louis office?"

"Yes."

"That explains it then."

"Explains what?" Wilkes asked, frowning.

"You're not Old Alan's type, but you are William's."

"And what type is that?"

Maddux studied Wilkes for a moment and then said, "If I told you that, Mr. Wilkes, it would ruin both our meals."

Maddux put his napkin down on the table and

stood up. "I'm going to take another turn around town." He assumed that Wilkes would take care of the check. Expenses were part of the deal.

As he was leaving the dining room he heard Wilkes asking Hannibal, "What did he mean by—"

Maddux smiled.

Thirteen

Walker Bogart's dominance over the town of Ceremony was spreading. By virtue of force he was already the most feared man in town. People stepped aside when he walked toward them, storekeepers served him without ever asking for payment, and even the law in Ceremony turned the other cheek when it came to Bogart and his men.

Part of Bogart's dominance was in being able to take over the largest house in town, which had formerly belonged to the mayor of Ceremony. Bogart had simply arrived on the mayor's doorstep one morning and announced that the house was his. The Mayor and his wife had then moved to the hotel. Mayor Perry had assured his wife that this was just a temporary situation.

"Just until we can figure out what to do about Bogart and his men, dear," he'd said.

"You and the others will continue to do what you've been doing," Janet Perry had said.

"What's that?"

"You'll let him walk all over you."

And, indeed, that was what Walker Bogart was doing, walking all over the people of Ceremony.

And to a man they were too frightened to do anything about it.

Walker Bogart walked into his house and nodded to the man he had watching the door. Inside, there was a man sitting in the living room, reading a newspaper.

"Where is she?" he asked.

"Upstairs," the man said.

"How is she?"

"Quiet."

"Has she eaten?"

"I brought her something a little while ago, but I don't know if she ate it."

"Has anybody touched her?"

"Geez, Mr. Bogart," the man said, "you told us not to, so we ain't."

"Good."

Bogart went upstairs to his bedroom, but she wasn't in there. He went to the other bedroom in the house and found Anne Redman there. She looked up as he came in, and there was no expression on her face. He saw the untouched tray of food on the top of the dresser.

"Miss Redman."

She didn't answer.

"You haven't eaten."

No reply.

"You should eat, you know," he went on. "You have to stay healthy."

No reply.

"If you don't eat you'll lose weight, and if you lose weight you won't do those clothes justice."

"You call these clothes?"

Bogart had gone to all of the saloon girls who worked in the town and asked them each for their most revealing piece of clothing. He'd then taken Anne Redman's clothes away from her and provided her with garments he'd appropriated from the saloon girls.

Anne Redman wore those garments only because her only other choice was to go naked. At the moment she was wearing a rather gaudy red corset with black nylon stockings and garters. It was the least revealing thing she could find to wear, but her creamy breasts still threatened to spill out of the top of the corset.

"Those are the clothes I've chosen for you to wear," Bogart said. "Of course, I wish you would alternate the clothing a little more. You've been wearing that same outfit for weeks."

"And I'll keep wearing it until you take it away from me."

"Well, I'll have to do that eventually. Will you eat this food?"

"No."

"I'll leave it here in case you change your mind."

He turned to walk out of the room and Anne sprang off the bed, took hold of the tray, and threw it after him. It missed him and struck the wall on the hall, spewing food all over the floor. Some of it did get on Bogart's shoulder, but his reaction was surprisingly calm.

Bogart looked into the room and said, "I'll send someone up to clean this mess. You'd better close your door, though, because if he sees you like that he might get some ideas."

Bogart was going down the steps when he heard the door slam.

Anne Redman was furious.

Some of her fury was directed at Walker Bogart, for forcing her to dress up like a whore, but most of her fury was aimed at herself. She'd been dogging Walker Bogart's trail for weeks, and had finally decided that she might need some help. What she had not known was that Bogart was on *her* trail by that time, and consequently she had been taken—and taken rather easily. They had been waiting for her at the livery stable when she'd tried to leave the town of Kent's Fork, to pick up Bogart's trail again. Bogart hadn't been with them, but they'd made it clear to her whose men they were, and where they were taking her.

She had felt all along that Bogart was headed for New Mexico. Bogart's men had taken her directly to Ceremony without blindfolding her or making any attempt to keep her from knowing where they were taking her.

She had assumed that this meant she was going to be killed.

And there were days when she wished they *had* killed her.

Walker Bogart had been immediately taken with her, and had decided to keep her. He'd set her up in this house, and forced her to dress up in whores' underwear. For any normal woman that would have been demeaning, but to a woman in her line of work it was . . . downright embarrassing.

The odd thing about Bogart was that he basically left her alone. He protected her from his men—who would have liked nothing better than to take turns raping her—and had never once touched her, or even tried to.

In fact, most of the time—in spite of the way he

forced her to dress—he treated her with an almost reverent attitude.

She thought he was mad, and expected him to kill her at any time.

The prospect of dying did not bother her so much. It was the damned waiting.

Fourteen

Maddux's second turn around town yielded him nothing but an opinion that there were certainly not many decent-looking women in New Moon. For a town with such a pretty name, he thought that a shame.

He went back to the hotel after dark and found Shadoweyes waiting in the lobby. This apparently did not sit well with the clerk, who kept throwing the half-breed nervous looks.

"Come on," Maddux said. "Let's get a drink and talk somewhere else."

Shadoweyes stood up and followed Maddux out.

"What did you see or hear?" Maddux asked.

"Nothing much."

They went to the saloon and walked to the bar. As soon as they entered they attracted attention as strangers in town. John Shadoweyes, in particular, drew disapproving looks.

Maddux knew trouble was coming, but he was looking for trouble just about now.

"Two beers," he said to the bartender.

"One beer," the bartender said. "We don't serve Indians."

"Does he dress like an Indian?" Maddux asked.

"Just because he dresses like a white man don't make him one," the bartender said.

"Two beers," Maddux said.

"One beer," the bartender said again. "I told you we don't serve Indians."

"He's not full-blooded Indian," Maddux said, half serious.

"That don't make no—" the bartender started, but Maddux reached out and took hold of the front of the man's shirt. He made no move to resist when Maddux pulled him halfway across the bar.

"I said draw him a beer."

As the man's left hand came out from below the bar Shadoweyes reached out and caught it by the wrist. In the man's hand was a billy club, which he'd intended to use on Maddux. Shadoweyes took it from his hand.

"Now," Maddux said, "draw two beers."

"The sheriff's gonna hear about this."

"I know," Maddux said. "I'm gonna tell him." He released the man and pushed him so that he slammed against the shelves behind him, rattling the bottles.

The man drew two beers and put both of them in front of Maddux. Maddux pushed one of the beers over to Shadoweyes, and they drank.

Maddux looked the place over through the mirror behind the bar. Once he and Shadoweyes were served their beers, the rest of the men in the place seemed to sense that the entertainment was over, and they went back to their conversations, or their games, or their flirting with saloon girls.

There was a table in the back that was empty, and Maddux gestured towards it with his beer. He and Shadoweyes went and sat down.

"Tell me," Maddux said.

"I talked to the children in the town."

"Ah," Maddux said. Shadoweyes had always gotten along with children.

"Children see everything, and will talk to anyone who is willing to listen."

"That's true," Maddux said. "Now what did they see?"

"Pop Wingate owned the General Store," Shadoweyes said. "The children say he hired a man to work for him before he was killed."

"How long before?"

Shadoweyes shrugged. "What do children know of time?"

"What happened to this man after Pop Wingate was killed?"

"He left town."

"What did the man look like?"

"The children I spoke to were mostly girls," Shadoweyes said.

Maddux thought that would have thrilled any of the townspeople or parents who'd seen Shadoweyes talking to their little girls. He hoped they weren't going to run into trouble over that.

"They said he had dark curly hair, nice eyes, and was very handsome."

Maddux frowned. "Was he young? Old?"

"To children," Shadoweyes said, "we are all old."

"That's great."

"They said he was not so old as Pop Wingate."

"All right, so we've got a man younger than the victim—let's say that makes him under fifty—with dark hair and nice eyes."

"And he is handsome."

"And handsome."

Shadoweyes looked across the table at Maddux and said, "It is not much."

"Hell," Kyle Maddux said, "it's a hell of a lot more than we had when we came here."

Fifteen

Maddux and Shadoweyes finished their beers and Maddux was trying to decide whether he should go up to the bar for two more when the sheriff walked in, followed by two deputies. The sheriff looked around the room until he spotted Maddux, and then approached the table. His deputies stayed at the door.

"Sheriff," Maddux said.

The sheriff looked at him, and then at Shadoweyes. "I thought Bert didn't serve Indians."

Maddux smiled. "Bert changed his mind. What can I do for you, Sheriff?"

"I just thought I'd check on you," the sheriff said. "You know, do my job."

"Why don't you sit down and have Bert bring three more beers?"

The sheriff licked his lips, then said, "Why not?" He turned and called to the bartender to bring three more beers, and then sat down.

"I'm glad you came here, Sheriff," Maddux said. "I have some more questions to ask you."

Maddux looked past the man to his deputies, who were still standing at the door. "Why did you bring your deputies?"

The sheriff looked over his shoulder for a second, then turned back. "We were just making our rounds."

"Together?" Maddux said. "Small town like this and it takes three of you to make rounds?"

"I . . . like to be careful . . . and your friend here was seen talking to some little girls a while ago."

"Is that so?"

"Their parents were worried."

"The same parents who let their children out on the streets late at night?" Shadoweyes asked.

The sheriff stared at Shadoweyes and said, "We got a safe town here."

Shadoweyes looked away from the man.

"What questions you got?" the lawman asked Maddux.

"We heard something about a man Pop Wingate hired before he was killed."

"Pop was always hiring drifters to work for him. There might have been one here when he was killed."

"You don't remember."

"I told you," the sheriff said, "that's old news to me."

"I see."

"I'm sorry I can't help you, Mr. Maddux," the sheriff said. He drank down his beer and stood up. He was about to leave when he said, "Say, are you the same Kyle Maddux who was marshal up in Cromwell for some years?"

"A lot of years."

"Yeah, well," the sheriff said, "I heard you was dead."

"As you can see," Maddux said slowly, "I'm not dead."

"Retired, then."

"Yes."

"Then why are you looking for this feller who's shooting people in the back?"

"Let's just say I don't like backshooters."

"You huntin' bounty now?"

"There isn't a price on the man's head that I know of."

"Maybe that's because nobody knows what the hell he looks like."

"Maybe that's why," Maddux agreed.

"Well . . . you know when you'll be leaving town?"

"More than likely in the morning."

"See if you can't keep your breed away from the kids in town until then, huh?"

Maddux was about to say something when the hand of Shadoweyes fell on his arm and squeezed.

"I'll do my best, Sheriff," Maddux said.

The overweight sheriff nodded and, waving at his two deputies to follow, left the saloon.

"Buffoons like that give the job a bad name," Maddux said.

Maddux and Shadoweyes stayed a little longer at the saloon. Maddux turned away the advances of one saloon girl. He had the feeling that she would rather have offered herself to Shadoweyes, but was afraid to.

On the way back to the hotel Shadoweyes said, "What do we do about the tail?"

"You know," Maddux said, "I've had a feeling— how long has he been with us?"

"Since we left Cromwell."

"Why didn't you say something before now?"

Shadoweyes looked at him and said, "I assumed you knew about it."

"I should have," Maddux said, chiding himself, adding with feeling. "I had a feeling, damn it, but I should have known."

"It has been a while since you were on the trail," Shadoweyes reminded him.

"Let's assume he's an observer," Maddux said, waving the excuse away. "He was probably sent to Cromwell to report on whether or not I had been killed. Since I wasn't, he is now just following us."

"Why doesn't he try to kill you?"

"Three men have failed, and now I'm traveling with three men myself."

"All right," Shadoweyes said. "What do we do now?"

"Well, as of now we do nothing," Maddux said. "We get some sleep and an early start. Tomorrow, one of us will hang back and see what kind of answers we can get out of our friend the observer."

"I will do it."

Maddux studied Shadoweyes for a moment, then decided that it was a good idea. Up to now it had been all Maddux could do to stay in the saddle. Sneaking up on someone was just not something he felt capable of doing—not just yet, anyway. "All right."

Maddux had no illusions that he was as good or as quiet as Shadoweyes, even in his prime.

Sixteen

Early the next morning Maddux banged on the door of Joe Hannibal's room. When the door opened he saw that Hannibal was dressed and ready. He hadn't spoken to Hannibal the previous night before turning in, so he was pleased to see that his friend had anticipated him.

"I figured you'd want to get a very early start," Hannibal said.

"Did you tell the city boy that?"

"I did," Hannibal said, "but we'd better bang on his door anyway."

"I'll do it," Maddux said. "Shadoweyes has already gone to the livery to get the horses ready."

"Did you find out anything else last night?"

"Yeah," Maddux said, "I'll tell you about it later."

Maddux went down the hall and banged on the door of Glenn Wilkes's room. When there was no immediate answer he forced the door open. The flimsy hotel lock did little to keep him out.

Wilkes was sprawled on the bed, fast asleep. Maddux looked around, saw the pitcher of water on the dresser, and couldn't resist.

He walked over, got the pitcher, and then very

deliberately poured the water over Wilkes's head.

Wilkes came up sputtering, looking around the room frantically.

"Wha—wha—" he blubbered.

"Let's go, Wilkes!" Maddux called out. "We don't keep bankers' hours out here, you know."

Wilkes sat up and glared at Maddux. "You—you didn't have to do that."

"Well, I knocked," Maddux said, "and I called and I shook. This was my last option before I fired my gun in your ear."

"Damn you."

"Look," Maddux said, "Hannibal told you we wanted to get an early start."

"Yes, but I expected someone to wake me up."

"Well, we don't have a wake-up service, Wilkes. Now, we're all ready to roll, so you only have a couple of minutes to get dressed . . . and dried."

Maddux turned to leave and Wilkes said plaintively, "What about breakfast?"

"You'll have to wait until lunch," Maddux said over his shoulder, and closed the door behind him.

Maddux, Hannibal, and Shadoweyes were mounted and ready to leave by the time Wilkes showed up at the livery. He was trying to control his breathing so that they wouldn't know that he had run from the hotel.

"Well, at least you saddled my horse," he said mounting up.

"Shadoweyes did it," Maddux said.

Wilkes didn't reply.

"I told him not to," Maddux said.

Again, Wilkes made no reply.

"You could say thank you," Maddux said.

Wilkes frowned at Maddux, then turned to Shadoweyes. He seemed about to say something when Shadoweyes kicked his horse in the sides and started forward.

"Let's go," Maddux said, and followed Shadoweyes out.

Now as they rode out of town Shadoweyes, who had taken the lead, rode further ahead of them, as if he were riding point. His plan was to ride far enough ahead to be able to circle back and come up behind the man who was following them.

Then he would ask him a few friendly questions.

Ed Chartman's back hurt. That came from sleeping in a doorway across the street from the hotel where Maddux and the others were staying.

Charterman had ridden to Cromwell with three of Walker Bogart's men, to observe while they tried to kill Maddux. After Maddux had shot the three of them, killing two, Charterman had sent a telegraph message for instructions—sending his message to a town in Texas, from where it was relayed to Bogart in New Mexico, so it couldn't be traced—and his instructions were to follow Maddux when he left, and keep an eye on him. If and when he started to get close, Charterman was to send word.

Charterman peered ahead now, making sure that he was close enough to follow, but not close enough to be seen. The terrain was mostly flat, with some stands of trees and rock formations, and he had to maintain a respectable distance to avoid being seen. Charterman was not a gunman, and was only kept around by Bogart to do menial tasks. He had felt that this job was a way to move up in Bogart's estimation, and he was determined to do it right.

Walker Bogart didn't like his men to make mistakes. When they did, they generally ended up dead, like the men in Cromwell.

Ed Charterman had no hankering to end up dead.

Seventeen

Hannibal rode up on Maddux and asked, "Where did Shadoweyes go?"

"He's going to ask our friend some questions," Maddux answered.

"Our friend?"

Maddux jerked his thumb behind them and Hannibal understood.

"What's going on?" Wilkes asked, riding up next to them on Hannibal's side. "I don't like being left out."

"Nobody's leaving you out, Mr. Wilkes," Maddux said.

"Where did the half-breed go?"

Maddux ignored him.

Hannibal said, "He has a name, Mr. Wilkes."

"I know he has a name, for Chrissake!"

Now he was ignored by both Maddux *and* Hannibal.

"All right," Wilkes said. "Where did Shadoweyes go?"

"We have a tail," Maddux said. "He's gone to find out what the man knows."

"A tail?" Wilkes asked, turning quickly in his

saddle to look back. "I don't see anything."

"He's far enough back so that you wouldn't."

"How long has he been there?"

"Since we left Cromwell."

"And you didn't know it?" Wilkes asked Maddux.

"Of course he knew it," Hannibal said. "He *and* Shadoweyes knew it."

"And the marshal," Maddux said.

"Well, that's fine," Wilkes said. "Everyone knew it but me."

"We all saw it on our own," Maddux said. "We didn't discuss it until we got to New Moon."

"And none of you did anything about it?"

"He was just watching us, Wilkes," Maddux said. "He was doing no harm so long as we knew he was there."

"And now?"

"Now we want to see if he knows where Walker Bogart is. Maybe he knows something about the Backshooter too."

Exasperated, Wilkes said, "There's no price on *his* head. We don't even know what he looks like."

"We have a partial description," Maddux said, and gave it to the man.

Wilkes stared at Maddux openmouthed, and then said, "And how long have we had *that?*"

"Since last night. Shadoweyes got it from some children in town."

"Children?" Wilkes said. "Oh, for Christ—"

"Mr. Wilkes," Hannibal said. "I'm a God-fearing man and I'd appreciate it if you didn't keep using the Lord's name in vain."

"Oh for—" Wilkes started, and then thought better of it. "Shouldn't we stop, or go back, or something?" he asked.

"No," Maddux said. "Shadoweyes will talk to the

man and then catch up with us.''

"Meanwhile, where are we headed?''

"Southwest, to the town where the Backshooter claimed his next victim,'' Maddux said. "That *is* where we want to go, isn't it?''

Ed Charterman didn't know what hit him.

One minute he was riding along on his horse, and the next he was sitting on the ground.

He looked up and saw an Indian dressed like a white man drop down from a tree. Obviously, the man had kicked him off his horse from up there.

Charterman had an idea of going for his gun, but the Indian spoke just then.

"Don't try it,'' Shadoweyes said.

Charterman looked at the gun on the Indian's hip and froze. He didn't know if the Indian knew how to use the gun or not. "What do you want?''

"Just some simple answers to some simple questions.''

"I don't know you.''

"You should,'' Shadoweyes said. "You have been dogging my trail—and the trail of my friends—ever since we left Cromwell.''

"Cromwell? I don't even know where that is.''

"We will not get anyplace if you continue to lie,'' Shadoweyes said. "If you do that I shall have to force the information from you.''

The man swallowed and eyed the Indian with fear.

Shadoweyes could see that this was not a brave man, and knew that he could find out what he wanted—if the man was also not a foolish man.

"I want to know about Walker Bogart,'' Shadoweyes said.

The man shook his head, closing his eyes.

Shadoweyes knew the man's quandary immediately. He was afraid of Shadoweyes, but he was also afraid of Bogart.

"I want to know about Walker Bogart," Shadoweyes said again.

"Jesus," the man said, "I can't—Bogart will kill me."

"I will not kill you," Shadoweyes said, "but I will make you long for death."

"But . . ." the man said again, and it was like a sob.

"Where are they?"

"N-New Mexico," the man said, almost blubbering now.

"Where in New Mexico?"

Charterman closed his eyes, and he could see Walker Bogart. If Bogart ever found out that he talked . . . he couldn't . . . he had to do something . . .

When the man opened his eyes Shadoweyes saw something there. "Don't," he said.

The man ignored him. His fear of Walker Bogart gave him the courage to draw his gun.

Shadoweyes was not a gunman, he did not possess fancy shooting skills. He did what he knew how to do. He drew his gun and fired first, the bullet going into the man's chest.

He looked down at the dead man and holstered his gun.

"Foolish."

Maddux heard the shot, as did Hannibal and Wilkes.

"What was that?" Wilkes said.

Maddux reined his horse in, and the others stopped behind him. It wasn't easy to tell, but he felt sure the shot had come from behind them.

He looked at Hannibal and the marshal said, "Shadoweyes can take care of himself."

"I know that," Maddux said. "I just hope he learned something before he killed the man."

"Killed him?" Wilkes said. "He was supposed to question him, not kill him."

"If Shadoweyes killed him," Maddux said, "he had a good reason for it."

Eighteen

Maddux, Hannibal, and Wilkes were camped when Shadoweyes caught up to them. They had found a formation in the ground that was almost like a small basin, and had scared up enough brush and chips to build a fire.

"Coffee's ready," Maddux said.

"I can use it," Shadoweyes said. "Let me settle my horse."

"I'll take it," Hannibal said.

Shadoweyes looked at Hannibal for a moment, then handed him the reins. He then accepted a cup of coffee from Maddux and hunkered down by the fire.

Glen Wilkes was sitting off to himself, and he was staring at Shadoweyes.

"What is wrong with him?"

"He thinks we're hiding plans from him."

Shadoweyes sipped the hot coffee without blowing on it first, the way a white man would. "You heard the shot?"

"Yes," Maddux said. "I figured you had your reasons."

"The best reason," Shadoweyes said. "A desperate man tried to kill me."

"Did he say anything first?"

"Yes," Shadoweyes said. "New Mexico."

"He didn't say where?"

"That was when he drew," Shadoweyes said. "He was more afraid of Walker Bogart than he was of me."

Maddux had beans on the fire and they were ready. He spooned some out and handed the plate to Shadoweyes.

"Come and get it!" he shouted to the others.

Glenn Wilkes came over grudgingly and spooned some into a plate for himself, then went back to where he had been sitting.

"He should do that more often," Shadoweyes said.

"What?"

"Stay off to himself."

Hannibal came over at that point. "The horse is taken care of."

Shadoweyes looked at him again, then said, "I thank you."

"Forget it. Let me get some of those beans." Hannibal helped himself, then sat back. "What did we find out?"

"We're going to New Mexico."

"Do we know where in New Mexico?"

"No," Maddux said. "The man pulled a gun and Shadoweyes had to kill him."

"Damn fool," Hannibal said. "But at least Shadoweyes here found out something. In fact, he's been finding out damn near everything."

"That's why I wanted him along."

Shadoweyes said nothing.

Hannibal looked at Maddux. "How are we going to play this?"

"You know what Bogart looks like?"

"Only from the poster."

"Yeah," Maddux said, "me too, and that could be anybody."

"We can't go riding around New Mexico asking if anybody's seen him," Hannibal said. "Word will get back to him faster than you can spit."

"We'll have to play it by ear," Maddux said. "We'll continue to dog the Backshooter's trail, because it will take us to the border of Mexico and West Texas. New Mexico's a hop, skip, and a jump from there."

"Maddux, I'm sorry to bring this up. . . ."

"Go ahead."

"What if Bogart is fishing . . . and he's got us hooked . . . and he's reeling us in."

"It's possible," Maddux said.

"Maybe he's after you."

"Me?" Maddux asked. "What the hell for?"

"Come on, Kyle," Hannibal said. "You put a lot of people away. And Bogart has been building himself a hell of a reputation for the past three years. If he draws you out of retirement and kills you—"

"A lot of people will be saying 'so what.'"

"I don't think so," Hannibal said. "I've got another question."

"Go ahead."

"If Walker Bogart *wants* you to come to him, why did he send three men to kill you."

"He didn't."

"What do you mean, he didn't? Then who were those three guys—"

"He sent three guys to *try* and kill me."

"Wait a minute," Hannibal said. "I'm just a poor dumb country lawman."

"Yeah," Maddux said, "you may be poor. Okay, let me explain it to you. I think Bogart sent them after me to see if three years of ranching had made me rusty. If it had, they would have killed me."

"And since they didn't, he knows you're coming for him."

"Well, wouldn't you?" Maddux said.

Hannibal leaned forward and said, "And what about Wilkes over there?"

Maddux shrugged and said, "There's a joker in every game, Hannibal."

"Yeah," Hannibal said, "but in some games the joker's wild."

Maddux laughed and said, "Not in any game I ever played."

Nineteen

"Why can't we go into town?" Glenn Wilkes complained.

"Because it's not on our list," Maddux answered.

"Look," Wilkes said, "I don't see why we can't go into town and sleep on real beds and eat a decent meal at a table with—"

"Joe," Maddux said, "See if you can explain to Mr. Pinkerton here," and walked away from the two men. Maybe Hannibal could talk some sense into Wilkes. Maddux was tired of trying.

"What is he complaining about now?" Shadow-eyes asked.

"He wants to sleep on a mattress."

"He should have brought his own." Shadoweyes smiled, then looked at the ex-lawman. "Maddux."

"What?"

"I know you don't believe in fate."

"So?"

"So this Glenn Wilkes shows up in Cromwell to ask for help in finding the Backshooter and, oh, by the way, maybe Walker Bogart too. At the same time Walker Bogart sends three men to kill you—or *try* and kill you. Now you figure Bogart *wants* you to find him."

Maddux stared at Shadoweyes.

"What is wrong?"

"That's the most I've heard you say at one time."

Shadoweyes frowned. "Who is Glenn Wilkes, Maddux? How do we know he is telling the truth?"

Maddux shrugged. "We'll let him go on for a while longer. As long as he's in front of us he can't hurt us."

"Whatever you say. I will just keep my eyes on him from now on."

"Well, that'll make me feel better," Maddux said, truthfully. "I wonder if him being such a pain in the ass is part of the act, or if it comes natural."

"It comes natural."

"What makes you say that?"

Shadoweyes gave Maddux a solemn look and said, "He is too good at it."

Shadoweyes cooked dinner that night, keeping one eye on the pan and the other on Glenn Wilkes. He was making beans, but he put some bacon in also. When the coffee was ready they all took a cup and drank it while waiting for dinner to be ready.

Wilkes went off and sat by himself while Hannibal pulled up a log by Maddux.

"What's with Shadoweyes?" he asked.

"What about him?"

"He's been watching Wilkes pretty closely."

"He doesn't like him."

"There's more to it than that."

"He doesn't trust him."

"That I can believe."

"He thinks it was too much of a coincidence that Wilkes appeared in Cromwell just when Bogart sent some men to try me."

Join the Western Book Club
and GET 4 FREE* BOOKS NOW!
A $19.96 VALUE!

Yes! I want to subscribe to the Western Book Club.

Please send me my **4 FREE* BOOKS**. I have enclosed $2.00 for shipping/handling. Each month I'll receive the four newest Leisure Western selections to preview for 10 days. If I decide to keep them, I will pay the Special Members Only discounted price of just $3.36 each, a total of $13.44, plus $2.00 shipping/handling ($19.50 US in Canada). This is a **SAVINGS OF AT LEAST $6.00** off the bookstore price. There is no minimum number of books I must buy, and I may cancel the program at any time. In any case, the **4 FREE* BOOKS** are mine to keep.

*In Canada, add $5.00 shipping/handling per order
for the first shipment. For all future shipments to
Canada, the cost of membership is $16.25 US,
which includes shipping and handling.
(All payments must be made in US dollars.)

NAME: _____

ADDRESS: _____

CITY: _____ **STATE:** _____

COUNTRY: _____ **ZIP:** _____

TELEPHONE: _____

E-MAIL: _____

SIGNATURE: _____

If under 18, Parent or Guardian must sign. Terms, prices, and conditions subject to change. Subscription subject
to acceptance. Dorchester Publishing reserves the right to reject any order or cancel any subscription.

"Well . . . Bogart could have heard he was coming to see you to get your help."

"How? Unless Wilkes isn't the Pinkerton he says he is."

"Then what is he?"

"We'll ask him, in due time."

"So what are we gonna do until then?"

"Exactly what Shadoweyes is doing," Maddux said. "We're gonna keep an eye on him."

Later, while Maddux was eating, Wilkes came over and sat by him.

"If you're gonna complain about the accommodations—" Maddux started.

"No, no," Wilkes said, "no complaints. I just have a question."

Maddux sighed and said, "What is it?"

"Shadoweyes."

"What about him?"

"He's been watching me all afternoon."

"Maybe he doesn't like you."

"I'm sure he doesn't," Wilkes said, "and that doesn't bother me at all, but somehow I don't think that's the reason."

"Then what do you think is the reason?"

"I don't know," Wilkes said, "unless he doesn't trust me, for some reason."

Maddux ate some beans and said, "John Shadoweyes doesn't trust too many people."

"He trusts you."

"Maybe that's because I'm the only white man he knows who doesn't look down on him."

Wilkes grinned and said, "Well, you certainly have him fooled, eh?"

Maddux turned his head slowly to look at Wilkes and said, "Wilkes, you'd better go back where you were sitting."

"Please," Wilkes said, "if he's your friend then I'm sorry I said anything. I certainly didn't come over here to offend you."

"He *is* my friend."

"Okay," Wilkes said. "He's your friend."

Wilkes took a forkful of beans, made a face, and swallowed. "Say," he said, "just out of curiosity, what kind of Indian is he anyway?"

"His mother was a Kiowa."

"Kiowa," he repeated. "Are they, uh, vicious . . . I mean, are they a warlike tribe?"

"Very," Maddux said. "They don't like white men at all."

"I see."

Wilkes looked over at Shadoweyes then and saw that the half-breed was staring at him.

"Well, if he hates white men, then how come he's not staring at Hannibal like he is at me?"

Maddux waited a beat, then said, "Some white men he likes less than others."

Twenty

Walker Bogart had taken over the Ceremony Saloon—literally taken it over. He had walked in with two of his men, entered the office of owner Jim Barnes, and told him that he was buying the saloon— and then given Barnes a dollar!

Bogart was sitting in "his" saloon, at a back table, enjoying the fact that the money all the people were spending was going into his pocket. He'd gotten rid of the bartender and put his own man behind the bar. He'd kept the four girls who worked there, though, and since they needed the job they'd stayed.

They'd also stayed because they were afraid not to.

Ginger, the oldest of the girls, a thirtyish redhead, went past, and Bogart put his big arm out to ensnare her and draw her into his lap. She put up some token resistance, but no real fight, as he buried his face between her big breasts.

At the bar Jerry Parnell said to the new bartender, Billy Cowen, "He's got that Redman woman back at the house and she makes any of these four look like cows. How come he paws these girls, but he doesn't touch her?"

"She's a lady," Cowen said.

115

Parnell snorted. "A lady? When did Walker Bogart ever treat a woman like a lady?"

"I guess this is the first time," Cowen said. He looked over at Bogart with Ginger in his lap and said, "I tell you, I wouldn't mind rubbing *my* face in that a little."

"Yeah," Parnell said, "neither would I—although this one's not bad either."

He grabbed one of the girls who was going by, a blonde named Maxie, and pulled her to him. She was about twenty, short and almost plump. He shook her a little and watched how her breasts jiggled.

"Look at that, will you?" he said to Cowen.

Maxie lifted her foot and brought her heel down on Parnell's instep. He howled, released her, and began hopping around. The man standing nearby began to laugh, and some began to clap in time with his hopping around.

"I ain't no stuffed toy," Maxie spat at Parnell. She turned to Cowen and said, "Give me two beers, Billy."

"Sure, Maxie."

Cowen drew two beers and put them on a tray for Maxie to deliver.

"Bitch!" Parnell said, ceasing his hopping and moving back to the bar. "I'll show her a thing or two."

"Yeah, well, before you do maybe you better give Bogart that news you was talking about."

"Yeah," Parnell said, "after I have another drink. Pour one, will you?"

Parnell picked up his drink, walked over, and stood in front of Bogart's table.

"You're blocking my view," Bogart said. "Sit down, for Chrissake!"

Parnell sat.

"What do you want, Parnell?"

"I have some news for you."

Bogart moved his eyes from the crowd to Parnell, who looked nervous. "You're nervous, Jerry," he said. "That means that I'm not going to like what you have to tell me."

"It's not my fault, Walker."

"Did someone touch her?"

"No, nothing like that," Parnell said. "We haven't heard from Charterman."

"Is that all?"

"We should have heard from him by now."

"So?"

"So he's probably dead, seeing as how he was dogging Maddux's trail."

"I repeat, so?"

"Well, we've got no one watching Maddux now, if Charterman's dead."

"So what?" Bogart said. "We know he's coming, don't we?"

"But how does he know where to come?"

"He'll figure it out," Bogart said. "If Maddux is so damned good, he'll figure it out."

Twenty-One

It was less than two months later when they rode into Kent's Fork, Texas, just a few miles from the Mexican border and the New Mexico border.

They put their animals up at the livery, got their hotel rooms, and then repaired to the saloon to wash away some trail dust and consider their next move.

This was the town in which the twelfth victim had been claimed. Traveling through Texas, from northeast to southwest, they had continued to ask questions in each of the towns where a victim had lived. In five of those places people recalled a dark-haired stranger coming to town, staying for a period of time, and then leaving after the murder. In one town he had gone by the name Bart Silver, in the other Billy Salt.

"We have a dark-haired man, thirty to forty, who has worked at a passel of jobs," Maddux said. "He has always been described as pleasant and well mannered. Whether or not we find out anything here, we're going to have to decide what our next move is, Mexico or New Mexico."

"New Mexico," Wilkes said.

"Why?" Maddux asked, even though he knew

the answer.

"Because that's where you said Bogart was—at least, he was a couple of months ago. He could be anywhere by now."

"That's true," Maddux said. Privately, he did not think so. He thought that Walker Bogart had probably dug in somewhere, waiting for him to come and get him.

He had decided that Hannibal was right. If Bogart could kill Maddux it *would* make his reputation. History would forget that Kyle Maddux was fifty-three and was suffering from a bad back. All history would show was that Walker Bogart killed Kyle Maddux.

If it happened that way.

Maddux was going to do his best to see that it didn't—but he wasn't going to go running headlong into Walker Bogart's arms. Let the man wait and wonder, and if he got tired of waiting, let him make the first move.

"Let's all move around town and see what we can find out," he said, standing up.

"I haven't finished my beer," Wilkes complained.

No one paid any attention to him. They had long since decided that this was the best way to handle him.

"How long we gonna wait, Walker?" Jerry Parnell asked.

"As long as I say, Parnell," Bogart said, staring across the table at Parnell.

"He ain't comin'," Parnell said.

"He'll be here."

"If he was comin' he would have been here by now," Parnell insisted. "We got to get moving."

"That's the reaction he wants," Bogart said.

"What?"

"He wants me to react the way you're reacting now," Bogart said. "He's a smart old man, that Maddux."

"Why do you have to kill him?" Parnell asked. "Why do we have to wait here for him, especially since he *is* an old man?"

"Because old or not, he's got a reputation," Bogart sid, "and I want it."

"You already *got* a reputation!"

"Sure, mine," Bogart said, "but I want to add *his* to it."

Parnell sagged in his chair, surrendering. He wasn't going to talk Bogart into leaving Ceremony. In fact, Bogart had so completely taken the town over that Parnell was starting to think he'd never leave. "What about the girl?"

"What about her?" Bogart asked.

"Well, the men are startin' to talk—"

"About what?"

"About what you're gonna do with her after all this time," Parnell said. "I mean, if *you* don't want her, we—I mean, they do."

Bogart, who had been sitting very relaxed in his chair at the saloon—sitting at *his* private table—now sat up and glared at Parnell.

"The woman is mine, Parnell," Bogart said. "Any man who touches her will have to face me. Do you understand?"

"Sure, Walker, sure, I understand," Parnell said hurriedly.

"And you'll make sure the others understand?"

"Sure, Walker, you know I will. You know you can count on me."

"Sure, Parnell," Walker Bogart said, sitting back,

"I know I can."

Parnell turned to leave and Bogart called out his name.

"Yeah?"

"You know that town where we picked up the girl?"

"Sure, Kent's Fork."

"Put a couple of men on the border near there."

"The Mexican border?"

"No, stupid," Bogart said, "the border between New Mexico and Texas."

"What are they looking for?"

"Jesus," Bogart said to himself, and then he barked at Parnell, "Figure it out!"

The sheriff at Kent's Fork remembered the stranger.

"Now that you mention it there *was* a stranger in town who fit that description," Sheriff Wade Miller said to Maddux.

"Did he know the victim?"

"Everybody in town knew Sam Rosen," Miller said, "but it sure didn't make any sense for anyone to kill him."

"Why not? Did he have a position in town?"

"Oh, he had a position, all right," Miller said. "He was the town drunk!"

"The town drunk?"

Miller nodded. "Why would anyone want to kill him?"

Maddux didn't have an answer. "Would you have any idea where the man went?"

"He was just gone the morning after the murder," Miller said.

"Excuse me for asking you this, Sheriff," Maddux

said, phrasing carefully, "but didn't it occur to you that this stranger might have been the killer?"

Miller stared at Maddux for a few moments, then said, "No," thoughtfully.

Maddux watched with interest as the man mulled over the suggestion.

"I mean," said Miller, "I couldn't understand why *anyone* would want to kill poor Sam, let alone a stranger who had only been in town a few days, but I never really figured anyone in particular for it."

Maddux frowned. This was a departure from what had happened in the other towns. Here the dark-haired Backshooter had not bothered to become acquainted with victim, and he had not spent as much time in Kent's Fork as he had in the other towns.

"All right, Sheriff," Maddux said, standing up. "Thanks for your time."

"Sorry I can't help you, Maddux," Miller said. "I don't even know the feller's name."

"That's all right," Maddux said. "We've got a ton of names for him, and it hasn't helped so far."

"Good luck," Miller said as Maddux left his office.

Twenty-Two

"All right," Glenn Wilkes said, "we're in New Mexico. Now what?"

They were camped one day into New Mexico and Shadoweyes was making some rabbit and beans for dinner.

"We just have to keep moving, Wilkes," Maddux said.

"Moving where?"

"I don't know."

"Tell me something, Maddux," Wilkes asked with some doubt. "Before you were retired were you *really* good at this?"

Wilkes was holding his plate out for Shadoweyes to fill. Shadoweyes spooned out some hot food and deposited it on Wilkes's exposed wrist.

"Ow, damn!" Wilkes said, pulling his scalded hand back. "You did that on purpose, you heathen!"

"I think it was an accident, Wilkes," Hannibal said.

"No," Shadoweyes said, "it was not."

"You see? What the hell is wrong with you, man?" Wilkes demanded of Shadoweyes.

"I am getting tired of you constantly digging at

Maddux, Mr. Wilkes," Shadoweyes said. "I thought someone should teach you some manners."

"By burning me?"

"It is something you will remember."

Maddux was watching carefully, thinking that the incident would go a long way toward showing them what kind of man Wilkes really was.

Shadoweyes stood up, inviting Wilkes to make a move on him.

Wilkes mistook the move and thought that Shadoweyes was going to take some action against him. "I have no gun."

"I do not need a gun," Shadoweyes said.

The two men regarded each other over the fire, and then Wilkes backed off. He leaned over and picked up his plate and made a show of trying to clean it.

Hannibal stuck his plate out and Shadoweyes filled it. Maddux was next, and then Shadoweyes looked at Wilkes expectantly.

"I'll get it myself," Wilkes said.

Shadoweyes shrugged, filled his own plate, and then left the spoon in the pan. Wilkes took his fill and then walked off to eat on his own.

"Nice move," Hannibal said to Shadoweyes.

"Thank you."

"I just had a horrible thought," Maddux said.

"What," Hannibal asked.

"If Wilkes is not who he says he is," Maddux said, "I don't think I'm going to get paid one red cent for this trip."

"Whoever he is," Hannibal said, "make him pay anyway."

"I guess I could do that."

"Besides," Hannibal said, "you're not doing this for the money anyway."

"Yeah," Maddux said, "good point."

After dinner Maddux said, "I think we should start

setting watches."

"Three?" Shadoweyes asked.

"We should make him take a turn," Hannibal said.

"Sure," Maddux said, " and then we'll take turns watching him."

In the end they set four watches, although Wilkes complained—as usual. Something about how his paying the way should earn him a good night's rest.

"We all pull our weight, Wilkes," Maddux said, "no matter who's footing the bill."

"Very well," Wilkes said, agreeing reluctantly.

Although Wilkes apparently had no handgun, he did have a rifle. Maddux told him to make sure he had it at hand while he was sitting watch.

They gave Wilkes the first watch, and then Maddux, Hannibal, and Shadoweyes put their bedrolls down in a row. They were each going to take an hour to watch Wilkes, waking each other up with a nudge for relief. This was to be done without Wilkes's knowledge. They didn't want him to know that they were watching him.

Not yet anyway.

Maddux was about to lie down when he saw that Wilkes was settling himself down in front of the fire.

"Don't sit in front of the fire."

"Why not?"

"If you sit and stare into the fire you'll have no night vision," Maddux explained. "Find a spot away from the fire."

"Jesus—" Wilkes said, but he got up and went to find himself a comfortable spot.

"And don't get too comfortable," Maddux said, before lying down.

Wilkes woke Maddux for the second watch. Mad-

127

dux had been asleep for two hours, having taken the first hour watch on Wilkes.

"Anything?" Maddux asked.

"What was I supposed to hear?"

"There should be some noise out there," Maddux said. "There are varmints out there, you know."

"Oh, I heard them," Wilkes said, with disdain. "I thought you were talking about two-legged varmints."

"Sometimes two-legged varmints can sound like four-legged varmints."

"Well, how the hell am I to know the difference?" Wilkes demanded.

Maddux shook his head, wondering if they should leave him off the watch.

"Go to sleep, Wilkes," Maddux said. "We're getting an early start in the morning."

"Are we going anywhere in particular?" he asked, sarcastically.

"There's a small town ahead of us a few miles," Maddux explained patiently. "We're going to stop there for supplies."

"Well, thank God," Wilkes said. "A real bed and real food."

"We may have a meal there, but we're not staying overnight."

"Why not?" Wilkes asked. When Maddux stared at him the man backed off and said, "All right, all right. Forget I asked."

Wilkes took his bedroll and set in on the other side of the fire, away from Hannibal and Shadoweyes.

Maddux walked away from the fire and found himself a rock to sit on. He hoped no one heard him groan as he sat down. His back was killing him after more than two months in the saddle, but he was happy to see that the other aches and pains—the ones that were a result of years of soft living—had subsided. His joints didn't ache so much anymore, and his ass didn't hurt as much.

Now if only the back pains would let up.

Sitting alone, he thought about Laura. He wondered if this trip, this search for a killer who shot his victims in the back, would be worth throwing away his marriage.

So far, it wasn't.

Parnell entered the saloon. Bogart was sitting with a drink on the table and a cigar in his hand. It was a position he seemed increasingly satisfied with. Parnell could remember a time when it was impossible for Walker Bogart to even stand still.

"What is it, Parnell?"

"The two men we had on the border?" Parnell said. "They just rode in."

"And?"

"Four men crossed into New Mexico not far from Kent's Fork."

"Is one of them Maddux?" Bogart's eyes glittered with eagerness.

"One of them is in his early fifties, the others are all younger," Parnell continued. "One is an Indian, the other two are white men. One's wearing a badge."

"Is the older man wearing a badge?" Bogart asked, frowning. Was Maddux coming after him with a posse—a posse of bounty hunters?

"No."

That satisfied Bogart for the moment that Maddux wasn't heading a posse, but he still had a lawman riding along with him.

"Tell me about the older one."

"He's tall, no gut, and like I said, in his fifties."

Bogart smiled around his big cigar and said with great satisfaction, "That's got to be him."

Parnell waited a few moments, then said, "He's got three men with him, Walker."

"I heard you."

"What do we do about them?"

"You and the others can kill them," Bogart said. "But make sure everyone knows—and I mean *everyone*, Parnell—that the old man is mine!"

"Don't worry, Walker," Parnell said, "they'll all know."

"It's gonna happen, Parnell," Bogart said, staring at something only he could see. "I can feel it in my bones."

Twenty-Three

The first town they came to in New Mexico was called Silver's Fork. Unlike Kent's Fork, this town took its name from an actual fork in the road. The fork was away from the town, but both parts of the fork led to the town. One just took longer than the other.

As they rode into Silver's Fork Glenn Wilkes looked around and said, "This is a town?"

"Well, it used to be," Maddux said. "Now it's just sort of a supply station for people entering New Mexico at this particular point."

"Does anyone live here?"

"Last time I was here it had a population of about fourteen. That includes the man who runs the general store and the fella who runs the saloon."

"You've been here before?" Wilkes asked.

"Many times."

"Then they know you."

"Yes."

"Well, maybe you could ask then about Bogart."

"Yeah, maybe I could."

Maddux reined his horse in and they all stopped.

"What's wrong?" Wilkes asked.

"I want to get something straight before we go into town."

"What?"

"*I* do the talking."

"Are you afraid I don't know how to talk?"

"I *know* you don't know how to talk to these people. Now, either you agree to keep quiet, or I'll have Shadoweyes cut out your tongue."

"You—you wouldn't dare," Wilkes said, looking at Shadoweyes.

"No, I probably wouldn't," Maddux said, "although I'm sure Shadoweyes would like it, but you get my point."

"Yes," Wilkes said, "I get your point."

"Good," Maddux said. "Just remember it."

They rode into Silver's Fork single file. Maddux, Hannibal, and Shadoweyes were on the alert for trouble, although they didn't really expect any. Bogart wasn't going to send men to every possible entry point. That would spread his forces too thin.

The buildings were all run-down wood structures, some boarded up and obviously empty, some not so obviously empty, and a few of them still open for business.

Maddux led them to the general store, where he dismounted.

"I'm going to go in here alone," Maddux said. "Why don't the rest of you go over to the saloon and I'll meet you there."

"Won't you need help with supplies?"

"I'm not going to buy that much. In fact, I think we should leave the pack animal here so we can travel more freely."

"What about our food?" Wilkes asked.

"We'll just have to eat less from here on in," Maddux said.

"I'll take the pack horse to the livery," Shadoweyes said.

"All right," Maddux said, "you do that. Divide the essential supplies among our four horses and put the animal up at the livery."

"Should I sell it?"

"If you can get a price, yes."

Shadoweyes nodded.

"Hannibal, take Mr. Wilkes over to the saloon and get him a drink."

"Right."

"I'd rather have something to eat," Wilkes was complaining as Hannibal led him away.

"Maybe they'll have some hardboiled eggs," Hannibal said.

Maddux entered the general store. Even though it had been a couple of years since he had last been through, he'd swear the same supplies were lining the shelves.

He walked to the counter and slapped his palm down on it, raising a small cloud of dust. After a moment the curtained doorway behind the counter belched forth a tall, gangly man with big ears and hands and a long jaw.

"Hello, Rufus," Maddux said.

Rufus Walter stared at Maddux for a moment, then said, "I'll be . . . Kyle Maddux."

"How are ya?" Maddux asked, putting out his hand.

Rufus took Kyle's hand in one of his huge ones. The man had the largest hands Maddux had ever seen. "How long has it been? A year?"

"More like three."

"Three? I heard you retired, someplace in Texas."

"Kansas."

"What brings you through here, then?"

"I'm looking for somebody."

"Anybody I know?"

"Walker Bogart?"

Rufus whistled soundlessly and said, "The worst. He's come a long way since you retired, Maddux."

"So I heard. I need some supplies, Rufus."

"Just tell me what you need."

"Some canned peaches, a pound of coffee, some beef jerky, beans, and some licorice."

"Licorice?"

"Doesn't take up much room and you can chew it for a long time."

"Licorice it is."

While Rufus was moving from shelf to shelf Maddux said, "What do you know about Bogart, Rufus?"

The man's back was to him but he saw his shoulders hunch for just a moment.

"Nothing much," Rufus said over his shoulder.

"Oh, come on, Rufus," Maddux said. "You know everything—especially everything that goes on in these parts."

Rufus put some supplies down on the counter and looked at Maddux. "I also know how to keep my mouth shut, Maddux," he said. "You know that."

"I do know that, Rufus, and I wouldn't ask if it wasn't important to me."

Rufus slumped and stared at Maddux.

"Rufus, I think Bogart wants me to find him."

Rufus thought about it, then said, "I can see that. He's done everything he can do to make a name for himself. Drawing you out of retirement, and then killing you . . . well, that would just about make him a legend."

"I don't know about a legend," Maddux said. "You have to kill a legend to become a legend."

"Don't underestimate your reputation," Rufus said.

"Well, are you gonna help me?"

"You want to know where Bogart is?"

"Yes."

Rufus thought a moment, then said, "I don't know exactly where he is, but I guess I can give you a general idea."

"Thanks, Rufus."

"Let me get you the rest of your supplies."

Maddux waited while Rufus collected all of his supplies, and then paid the bill. He had Rufus write out a receipt so he could give it to Wilkes.

"Rufus, you been reading the newspapers?"

"Sure," Rufus said, "but by the time I see them they're usually a couple of months old."

"That wouldn't matter," Maddux said. "You been reading about this fellow likes to shoot people in the back?"

"Oh, yeah, I read about that."

"You know anything about it?"

"Like what?"

"Like who he is maybe? Like if he's been through here? Like whether or not he works for Bogart?"

"I don't know any of that, Maddux," Rufus said. "I'll tell you all I know, though, you can count on that."

"Okay, Rufus," Maddux said, folding his arms, "I'm listening."

Twenty-Four

When Maddux entered the saloon, Hannibal and Wilkes were seated at a table with a beer in front of each of them. Maddux went to the bar and said, "Beer."

There were a few more tables scattered around the room, and in one corner some two- and three-legged tables and chairs were stacked like so much firewood.

"Hello, Maddux," the bartender said, putting the beer on the bar.

"Toke, how are you?"

"Could be better."

Toke Marlowe was sixty if he was a day, but he could have passed for eighty easy—or maybe it was the other way around. As many years as Maddux had been passing through here, Toke was always behind the bar, and they always had the same exchange.

Maddux took his beer over to the table and sat. "Shadoweyes must be dickering," he said.

"You find out anything interesting?" Hannibal asked.

Maddux took a moment to sip his beer. It was as cold as he remembered. Possibly the best beer he'd ever drunk was right here in Silver's Fork.

"Yeah, I found out something interesting," Maddux said. "It seems Walker Bogart has taken himself a town."

"What do you mean, taken?" Wilkes asked.

"Just what I said," Maddux replied. "He's taken the town."

"You mean . . . a whole town?"

"Sure," Hannibal said, "he's got enough men to do it."

"Well, what do we do now?" Wilkes asked. "What's the name of the town?"

"That we don't know," Maddux said, "but we do know that it's west of here."

"So we just ride west?" Wilkes said.

"He's learning," Hannibal said to Maddux.

"There's something else."

"What?" Hannibal asked.

"Some of Bogart't men were through here some months ago, maybe three."

"So?"

"They had a woman with them," Maddux said, "and she wasn't along willingly."

"Oh, that's fine," Hannibal said. "What do you think Bogart and his wild bunch will have done to that woman by now?"

"I don't even want to think about it."

"What are we worried about some woman for?" Wilkes asked.

"If Bogart has a woman and is holding her against her will," Hannibal said, "it will be up to us to get her away from him."

"Why?" Wilkes asked.

"Because," Maddux said, and when he didn't elaborate, Wilkes just frowned even more.

"Well, all right," Wilkes said, finally. "I mean, if we take Bogart, that'll set her free anyway."

Maddux didn't reply. For the first time since he knew him, Wilkes had said something that made sense.

Maddux was about to get up and go looking for Shadoweyes when the half-breed walked in. "What happened?"

"The liveryman wanted to buy, but he didn't want to pay a fair price."

"That would be old Jeff Kanaly," Maddux said. "What happened?"

"We dickered," Shadoweyes said, "and we finally agreed on a price."

"If you beat him I'll be impressed."

Shadoweyes stared at Maddux and then said, "You did want to get rid of the animal."

"Well," Maddux said, "as long as you got a *decent* price. Get yourself a beer."

Shadoweyes went to the bar and came back with a beer. Maddux told him what he had just told the others.

"Then we have a definite direction," Shadoweyes said.

"Yes," Maddux said.

"Then we leave?"

"We leave," Maddux said, "but there's something we've got to clear up first."

When neither Maddux nor Shadoweyes asked, Glenn Wilkes said, "What's that?"

"We may be in a little trouble where this Backshooter is concerned."

"How's that?" Hannibal asked.

"It's been two months since his last victim in Kent's Fork, and we just left that town."

"So?" Wilkes asked.

"So, we may have a direction on Bogart, but we've got nothing on this other boy."

"So then we go after Bogart," Wilkes said, "and forget about the other one."

Maddux shifted in his chair, trying to ease the pain in his back. "I'm not about to forget someone who shoots people in the back," he said.

"What do you want to do, Kyle?" Hannibal asked.

"I don't know," Maddux said. "I guess what I *don't* want to have to do is wait for him to take his next victim."

Kyle," Hannibal said.

"I know, I know," Maddux said. "that's about what it's gonna take for us to get a bead on him again."

Maddux sat sipping his beer, with the others all watching him.

"So?" Wilkes said, the first to become impatient. "What do we do now?"

Maddux turned his head and looked at Wilkes. "Let's clear something else up."

"Like what?" Wilkes asked.

"Like just who the hell you are, and what you're doing here."

Glenn Wilkes stared at each of them in turn, and for a moment Maddux thought he was going to try to go on with the pretense.

But he didn't.

"All right," Wilkes said, "my name *is* Glenn Wilkes."

"And?" Maddux said.

"And I am a Pinkerton agent," Wilkes said. "You saw my identification."

"Get to the parts you lied about," Maddux said.

Wilkes looked at the three of them again and then sighed and said, "I'm not after the Backshooter."

"Pinkerton wasn't hired by one of the families?" Hannibal asked.

"No."

"I figured that," Maddux said.

"How?" Hannibal asked.

"I've talked to the families of six of the victims, and none of them hired Pinkerton."

"What about the other six?"

"Three of them had no family, and the families of the other three had left town, and they didn't figure to have that kind of money."

"So what are you after?" Hannibal asked Wilkes.

"The reward on Bogart."

"The five thousand dollars?" Hannibal asked.

"No," Wilkes said, "the paper you have is outdated. The bounty on Bogart is fifteen thousand." He took a folded-up poster from his back pocket and put it on the table.

"Fifteen thousand?" Hannibal repeated in awe, picking up the poster. He unfolded it, then showed it to Maddux, who nodded. He passed it to Shadow-eyes, who couldn't read, so he just handed it back to Glenn Wilkes.

"If you're hunting Bogart," Maddux said, "why the pretense? Why get me involved?"

"I've heard Alan Pinkerton talk about you, Maddux," Wilkes said. "I knew that the Back-shooter's trail started in Kansas, and I knew you'd been shot in the back."

"How'd you know that?"

"Like I said," Wilkes said, "Pinkerton. He was always saying he wouldn't be surprised if you took off after this fella sooner or later."

"So you decided to play on that to get me to go with you?"

"Sure," Wilkes said. "Hey, this is your contry, Maddux. I'd be lost out here without you. I mean, listen, I was going to split the reward with you."

"Five thousand dollars," Maddux said.

"What?"

"You were gonna split five thousand dollars with me, right?"

"Well . . . no, I was going to split the entire reward with you."

"And what did you figure as a fair split?"

Wilkes fidgeted. "Well, I figured we'd splilt down the middle."

"Two ways?"

"Sure, you, me."

"And what about Hannibal and Shadoweyes?"

"Well," Wilkes said, fidgeting some more, "I didn't expect them to come along. I guessed you'd pay them from your share."

Maddux remained silent for a moment, then finished his beer before speaking.

"Here's the way I figure it," Maddux said. "We could leave you here and go on without you, and when we find Bogart we could split the reward three ways."

"You'd leave me out?" Wilkes demanded, outraged.

"Well, that's just one way of doing it," Maddux said.

"And what's another?" Wilkes asked suspiciously.

"We all leave here together," Maddux said, "and when we find Bogart we split four ways."

"*Four* ways?"

"Even split," Maddux said.

"Sounds fair to me," Hannibal said.

"I'm not done yet," Maddux said. "After we split the reward four ways, you're going to pay me for my time out of your share."

"What?"

"That way," Maddux said, "you'll still come out

with something."

"That's not fair!" Wilkes said. "I brought you into this."

"By lying to me," Maddux said. "Usually, when people lie to me, it gets real expensive. You're getting away cheap."

"Cheap, hell—"

"Or we could go back to the first option," Maddux said. "That way you'd get nothing."

"All right," Wilkes said, waving his hands. "Let's go back to the second option. I mean, four ways that still comes to three thousand seven hundred and fifty dollars—"

"He did that in his head," Hannibal said sarcastically.

"—and then how much is your fee?"

"I'll set my fee when the job is done," Maddux said. "I mean, if we all get killed, there's no use in my setting it now, is there?"

"Killed?"

"Killed," Maddux said. "That's the third option, and that way we all lose."

Wilkes looked away nervously.

"Tell me something else, Wilkes," Maddux said. "What?"

"Just how good a detective are you?"

"Well . . . I'm pretty good, I guess."

"Well, I hope you're a better detective than you are a bounty hunter."

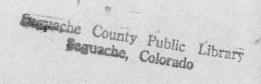

Twenty-Five

They left the saloon together and walked back over to the general store, where they'd left their horses. There were white sacks hanging from each saddle, with each man's share of the supplies to carry.

"Do you know how to use that rifle?" Maddux asked Glenn Wilkes.

"Sure I do."

"And do you have a handgun?"

Wilkes nodded. "In my saddlebag."

"Well, put the damned thing on. We're going to need every gun we've got."

They all mounted up, and Maddux turned towards Wilkes again. "I've got one more thing to say to you, Wilkes."

"What?"

"You lied to me, and you got caught at it." Maddux waggled his finger in Wilkes's face to keep him from cutting in. "That means that every time you open your mouth to me from now on, you might be lying to me again."

"I wouldn't—"

"Shut up!" Maddux snapped. "That means that from now on you speak only when you're spoken to, understand?"

"I don't—"

"Understand?"

Wilkes lapsed into silence, his eyes wandered around a bit, his face flushed, and then he said, "Yes, I understand."

"That's good," Maddux said. "Now let's ride."

By the time they'd put ten miles between themselves and Silver's Fork, Maddux had made up his mind about Glenn Wilkes. He was a leech, a parasite. Maddux had known his type before, bounty hunters who would think nothing of stealing from another bounty hunter, given half a chance. He saw a chance to make some money, and he wasn't above using another man to do it.

Maddux would have to watch Glenn Wilkes even more carefully now that he knew what he was, and he knew that Hannibal and Shadoweyes were thinking the same thing.

When they stopped that night to camp, Wilkes sat at the fire with Maddux and Hannibal. It was Shadoweyes who went off on his own to eat this time.

"So that's why Shadoweyes was watching me so intently," Wilkes said.

"Why?" Maddux asked.

"Because he didn't trust me."

"None of us did," Maddux said. "In fact, none of us do."

"Hey—"

"I'd be very careful about what I say and do for a while, Wilkes," Maddux said. "Real careful."

"I told you fellas the truth."

"Sure, after we demanded it," Maddux said. "Would we have heard it otherwise?"

146

"Well, you would have had to hear it once we found Walker Bogart."

"Sure."

Wilkes fell silent.

"How would you collect the reward without us knowing about it? You haven't figured that part out yet. Had you, Wilkes?"

Wilkes hesitated, then said, "No. I didn't know what I was going to do when we found Bogart. I . . . don't know how to collect a bounty."

"That shows what an amateur you are," Hannibal said. "You've got know what you're going to do every step of the way in any plan you make."

"I'm an amateur, huh?" Wilkes said. "And what are you, some small-town lawman? What do you know?"

Hannibal fixed Wilkes with a hard stare and said, "I wasn't always a small-town lawman."

"Oh yeah, well—"

"That's enough, you two," Maddux said. "When we find Bogart and his men we're going to have to depend on each other. Let's not say some things we're gonna be sorry for later."

Hannibal and Wilkes fell silent, eating and occasionally looking across the fire at each other.

After they'd eaten, Maddux set up the same watches. Wilkes was first.

Twenty-Six

Walker Bogart now owned the mayor's house, the biggest saloon in town, the local cathouse—with free access to the girls, of course—the livery, and now he had his eye on the bank.

"I won't have it," Douglas Bent, the president of the bank, said. "We have to call in some help."

"What kind of help?" Mayor Perry asked. "Gunmen? Do you know how many gunmen we'd need?"

Jack Barnes said, "Well, something has to be done. I want my saloon back."

"Well then, go and tell him," Perry said.

"Sure, and you go and tell him you want your house back," Barnes said.

"I'm not the one who's complaining, Jack."

"Oh? You like living in the hotel?"

"There are worse things," Perry said. "He could have killed us all."

"Sometimes I wonder if that *would* really have been worse," Sam Amory said. He had been the owner of the livery before Bogart "bought" it for a dollar.

"Come on," Perry said. "Dying is always worse."

"This whole town is dying," Jack Barnes said.

"We were growing by leaps and bounds, and now with Bogart here we're stagnant."

"Maybe," Perry said, "he'll just go away, eventually."

"All by himself," Barnes said. "Do you really believe that?"

Perry hesitated, then said, "Damn it, no."

"Where are they?" Bogart asked Parnell.

"In the town hall," Parnell said. "That's where they hold their town council meetings."

Bogart ignored Parnell's sarcasm. "All right," the big man said, "let's go to a town council meeting."

The four members of the town council were startled when the door to their meeting hall slammed open and Walker Bogart walked in, followed by his man Parnell.

"Well, well," Bogart said, "what have we here?"

"This is a town council meeting, Bogart," Mayor Perry said.

"So?"

"You're not on the council."

"You mean I wasn't on the council . . . until now," Bogart said.

He walked over to where Perry was sitting, at the head of the table, and loomed over him.

"Now I am a member," he said. "In fact, I think I'll be the chairman of the council. Would that be the chairman's seat you're in, Mayor?"

Perry had to try twice before he said, "Y-yes, it is."

"Then I'd like it, please."

Perry hesitated, and then stood up and moved to one of the other chairs at the table. Bogart sat down in the vacated chair and regarded the other members of what was now a five-man council.

"Now what were we discussing?"

No one answered.

"It wouldn't by chance have been how we could rid the town of some of its more . . . negative influences, could it?"

Again, no reply.

"Well, if we have nothing further to discuss, then," Bogart said, "I declare this meeting to be ended."

He made a show of looking around the table for something, and then said, "A gavel. I don't have a gavel so I can call meetings to a close. Parnell?"

"Yeah, Walker?"

"Make a note. I have to get a gavel for future town council meetings."

"I'll make a note, Walker."

"Gentlemen," Bogart said, drawing his gun, "in the absence of a gavel this will have to do. I now declare this meeting . . . adjourned."

He punctuated the remark by firing the gun.

Anne Redman heard the shot, and since she was already sitting in front of the window she saw the men running from the town hall.

Apparently, Walker Bogart had declared himself mayor, or leader of the town council, or something.

She watched as Parnell came out of the hall, followed by Bogart himself, who seemed to be laughing.

She was amazed that Bogart still had not touched her. She wondered how much longer that could go on. The man's eyes were like fingers on her whenever he was in the room. Surely he wouldn't be able to contain himself for much longer—especially if he

151

kept taking clothes away from her. She was now reduced to wearing a very flimsy red nightie through which she—and Bogart, and all of his men—could see her dark nipples and the firm curves of her breasts. She saw the way Bogart's men looked at her. How long would it be, she wondered, before someone decided to go ahead and try to rape her?

How long before her almost naked charms made one of Bogart's men forget that he was afraid of his boss?

How long would it be before Bogart himself decided to have her by force, instead of waiting for her to offer herself willingly?

She knew that she would never do that, and as soon as Bogart realized it, her time would be up.

Still, she sat in front of that window, waiting for somebody to come riding to her rescue.

She looked inside herself at that moment as something occurred to her. Maybe she should be working on a plan to get herself out, despite the fact that the town was full of Bogart's men.

There had to be a way.

All she had to do to find it was stop thinking like a victim and start thinking like what she was.

An experienced bounty hunter!

Twenty-Seven

Every town they came to, they decided that one of them should first ride in and take a look around. If it looked all clear, then he would signal to the others and they could ride in. This way the same person wouldn't always be seen asking questions.

Even Glenn Wilkes, although reluctantly, had done it once.

Once they were in town they would split up and go to the saloons, barber shops, and restaurants and just listen to the conversations that were going on. You could learn more from just listening than you could from asking questions, sometimes.

"Somebody's got to know something," Maddux said. "A man cannot take over a whole town with a gang of men and not have word get out."

They were in the saloon in a town called Wadsworth.

"Maybe we're just not close enough to where it's happening," Hannibal said. "We'll just continue to ride south and see what happens."

Was he getting impatient? Maddux wondered about himself. After three years out of the business, had he lost that most valuable commodity of patience? The very thing that had made him as good as he was?

"You're right," Maddux said. "We just keep riding, and we keep listening."

"I don't know if I have the patience for this," Glenn Wilkes said, and just hearing the man say that seemed to strengthen Maddux's own resolve.

"If you don't have the patience, Wilkes, you can always walk away."

"You'd like that, wouldn't you?" Wilkes said. "You'd like me to ride away and leave a full share behind, wouldn't you?"

"Wilkes," Maddux said, "I'd just like you to ride away, period. Hell, I'd even send you your share."

"Sure," Wilkes said, "sure you would. Well, I'm sticking around to look after my interests, and that's that."

"Then do it quietly," Maddux said.

Wilkes opened his mouth to answer, but thought better of it.

"What's the next town?" Hannibal asked.

"They said in the last town that the next one is called Dennison."

"Sometimes I wonder where people get the names for these towns," Hannibal said.

"Look who's talking," Maddux said. "Cromwell?"

"Hey, Cromwell is a *fine* name for a town," Hannibal said in defense of the people who had named the town where he was marshal—even though he wasn't there when they did it.

"Do I have to listen to you two argue about the names of towns?" Wilkes said.

"Wilkes," Maddux said, "if you were sitting somewhere else, you wouldn't have to listen to anything we say."

"All right, all right," Wilkes said, standing up, "I'll go and sit over there." He started to walk away, and then realized that Shadoweyes was sitting over *there*. "I'll sit over there," he said, and walked the other way.

"What are we gonna do with him?" Hannibal asked.

"I've been thinking about that a lot and I don't rightly know what we should do," Maddux said. "What do you suggest?"

"Well, you're not really going to give him a share of the reward, are you?"

"Why not?" Maddux said. "How else is he going to pay me what he owes me?"

"Well, what about me?" Hannibal said.

"What about you?"

"I can't take any of that reward. I'm an officer of the law."

"*Officially* you can't take any of the reward," Maddux said. "I'll give you some, don't worry."

"I don't know if I want it."

Maddux studied Hannibal's face and saw that he was serious.

"Well, if you don't, I'll hold it for you," Maddux said. "Someday you might need it."

"What about Shadoweyes?"

"What about him?"

"Does he need the money?"

"Probably not," Maddux said. "He's got everything he wants, but I'll hold his share too, in case he ever needs it."

"You'd do that, wouldn't you?"

"Do what?"

"Hold over seven thousand dollars in cash and never spend it, just in case we ever want it."

"No."

"No?"

"No, I wouldn't do that," Maddux said. "I'd put it in the bank and let it collect interest."

Wilkes took the first watch, and Maddux the first watch on Wilkes.

When Wilkes woke Maddux for the second watch he stayed up and had a cup of coffee with him.

"You know, you fellas don't have to keep watching me," he said.

"Why not?"

"Because we're partners in this," Wilkes said. "Partners have to trust each other."

"If we were partners, then you wouldn't owe me any money, and you do."

"You mean you're gonna hold me to the deal we made?"

"I made that deal in good faith," Maddux said, "even if you didn't, and yes, I'm going to hold you to it."

"You know, I really figured when you saw the size of the reward you'd be a little more understanding."

"When I retired from this business—the man-hunting part of it," Maddux said, "I meant to stay retired. You made me break my word to myself."

"For money."

Briefly, Maddux gave the man a humorless, almost pitying smile. "No, not for the money."

"So then what brought you out of retirement?" Wilkes demanded.

"Certainly not your offer."

"Why'd you take my offer, then?"

"Because I figured if I was going to go looking for the Backshooter," Maddux explained, "I might as well let you foot the bill."

156

"You know, I've heard a lot about you—"

"Then you know I mean what I say," Maddux said, fixing Wilkes with a hard stare.

"Yeah," Wilkes said, after a moment. He dumped the rest of his coffee into the fire and said, "Yeah, I know you mean what you say. Don't worry, Maddux, I'll hold up my end."

"That's good, Wilkes," Maddux said, "that's real good."

Twenty-Eight

Dennison was like a lot of New Mexico towns, small and just marking time.

Hannibal had gone in first and had found the town clean, so he'd ridden back to the town boundary and signaled the others to come ahead. Now they all rode down the main street to the livery stable.

"I never saw so many nothing towns in a row in my life," Wilkes said.

"New Mexico has its share of large towns," Maddux said. "We just haven't been traveling that route."

They left their horses at the livery and went in search of the saloon. It was midday and there were only a few patrons there drinking. They each got a beer from the bartender and took them to a table.

"We're not going to find out much here," Hannibal said, looking around.

"We might have to stay overnight," Maddux said, "maybe get into a poker game later."

"A poker game?" Wilkes said.

"Lots of gossip in a poker game, Wilkes," Maddux said. "You play much?"

"No, I don't."

"Why not?"

"I was never very good at it."

"Well then, I guess I'll do the playing," Maddux said. "Unless . . ." he added, looking at Hannibal.

"My poker-playing days are long gone," Hannibal said.

Maddux didn't bother asking Shadoweyes. The only poker the half-breed ever played was pass-the-time two-handed poker with Maddux.

"I guess we ought to get some hotel rooms," Hannibal said.

Hannibal looked at Wilkes and asked, "You still want your own room?"

Wilkes looked at Shadoweyes doubtfully and Maddux said, "Don't worry, you can share a room with me."

"Okay," Wilkes said. "I mean, I don't want to be difficult."

"Since when?" Hannibal said.

Hannibal seemed to be especially peeved at Wilkes, because Wilkes's deception had begun with fooling the marshal of Cromwell.

"Now look—" Hannibal said.

"Let's hold it down, shall we?" Maddux said.

"I'll go and see about the rooms," Hannibal said, standing up.

"I will take a walk around town," Shadoweyes said, also rising.

As they left Wilkes said, "I'm getting a little tired of being treated like I got the plague or something."

"You brought it on yourself," Maddux said. "Don't expect to come out of this thing with a lot of friends."

"As long as I come out with some money."

"You should be worried about coming out of this with a whole skin."

"Hey," Wilkes said, "I got the best manhunter in the business as a partner. Why should I worry?"

"Just remember," Maddux said, "I've been out of action for three years."

"I saw you in action in Cromwell, Maddux," Wilkes said. "You ain't lost a step."

"How would you know?" Maddux said. "You didn't see me three years ago—or ten years ago."

Maddux watched Wilkes's face as he digested the words, and was satisfied to see a small worry frown crease his brow.

Maddux hung around the saloon until early evening. By that time there were enough townspeople and cowboys in the saloon for someone to suggest a poker game, and he worked his way into it.

Wilkes took up a position at the bar and watched.

"Five-card draw is the game," one man said, explaining the rules. "No wild cards. Jacks or better to open, three-raise limit. Stakes are whatever you've got on you."

"Check and raise?" Maddux asked.

The man looked at him and then smiled and said, "Yeah, we check and raise."

It seemed that at least two or three of the men played regularly. In fact, Maddux was probably the only stranger to the game, which was at the moment five-handed.

The man who had explained the rules was Taggett. The other three men in the game were Gable, Crawford, and Mandon. Taggett and Crawford came from the same ranch, while Gable and Mandon were town merchants.

Maddux had been hoping to find a drifter or two in the game, men who were perhaps working their way north and who might have some news. As it turned out, this game was the only game in town.

He played for an hour, staying even. The big winner seemed to be Taggett, who kept up a steady chatter in between hands and while he dealt, but fell silent after all the cards were dealt out.

During the second hour of the game Hannibal walked in and positioned himself at the bar, away from Wilkes. Shadoweyes had still not reappeared.

During the third hour Maddux finally decided to say something about the game.

Maddux had been dealt a pair of aces, but he hadn't had a chance to open because Taggett had, while Crawford was dealing. Maddux called for three cards, and drew a third ace. Taggett announced he was breaking openers and made a one-card draw.

"Opener bets twenty," Taggett said.

Mandon and Gable dropped, and Maddux raised. Crawford, the dealer, dropped out.

"See your twenty, and raise forty," Taggett said.

"Your forty," Maddux said, " and raise forty more."

"Last raise is mine, I guess," Taggett said. "Your forty, and two hundred."

Maddux counted the money he had on the table and it didn't add up to two hundred.

"Well?" Taggett said.

"I'm going to call," Maddux said, "but first I want to ask you a question."

"What?"

"You fellas always cheat?"

The action at the table stopped and everyone stared at him.

"Who are you talking to?" Mandon asked.

"These two," Maddux said, indicating Taggett and Crawford.

162

"They're cheatin'?" Gable asked.

"You better be sure about what you're saying, fella," Tagget said.

"Oh, I'm sure," Maddux said. "See, you just split openers, and I don't think you had openers."

"What?"

"I think if we look at your hand, and at what you discarded, we'll see that you didn't have openers, so you opened illegally—and then he dealt you the card you needed for your straight, or your flush, which-ever you have."

Mandon looked at Taggett and said, "Is that true?"

Taggett ignored Mandon.

"You're startin' trouble because you can't call the raise," Taggett said. "You better be ready to back it up, friend."

"I am," Maddux said. "You call it."

Mandon and Gable stood up and moved away from the table. Crawford started to get up and Maddux said, "Don't move."

"I ain't got a gun, mister," Crawford said.

"Just stay there."

"He made me do it," Crawford said, whining now.

"Sit."

By now they had the attention of everyone in the saloon, and Maddux hoped that someone had been smart enough to send for the sheriff, and that the law would arrive before he had to kill someone.

"Look," Maddux said, "a card game is a poor reason to die."

"Ha! You're backin' down."

"No, I'm not," Maddux said. "I want you to."

"You called me a cheater, friend."

"And I can prove it."

"If you live that long."

"He will," Joe Hannibal said, and put his gun to

Taggett's head.

Taggett's eyes went wide, his back stiffened, and he said, "This ain't fair."

"I'm saving your life, mister," Hannibal said. He reached over Taggett's shoulder to turn over his cards. He had a heart flush.

Maddux reached across the table and turned over his discard, which was a five. It matched the five in Taggett's hand, which meant that he had opened on a pair of fives in a game where you needed at least a pair of jacks to open.

"Like I said," Maddux said, looking at Crawford, "do you fellas always cheat?"

"How do you like that?" Mandon said. "They *was* cheating."

"The pot's yours, mister," Gable said.

Maddux put down his three aces and raked in his pot. At that point the batwing doors opened and the sheriff came walking in.

"What's going on?" he demanded.

"Why don't we take these two fellas over to your jail, Sheriff," Hannibal said, "and I'll explain."

Twenty-Nine

For the first time since they left Cromwell, the fact that Joe Hannibal was a lawman came in handy. It got them some professional courtesy from Paul Fane, the sheriff in Dennison.

"So my friend was playing poker and spotted these yahoos cheating," Hannibal finished.

"I see," Fane said. "Well, we'll give them a one-way ticket out of town, and I'll talk to Big Mike Sideman, the man they work for. I don't think he's gonna want any card cheats workin' for him."

"Thanks for your help, Sheriff," Hannibal said, standing up and extending his hand.

Sheriff Paul Fane stood up and accepted the proffered hand.

"Anything else I can do for you while you're in town?" Fane asked.

"I don't think so, Sheriff," Hannibal said. "We'll be leaving in the morning."

"Where you headin'?"

"Don't know exactly. We heard there was a town somewhere hereabouts that's been taken over by a fella name Walker Bogart, but we haven't been able to find it."

"Why are you lookin' for it?" Fane asked. "Doesn't sound like the kind of a place for a visit."

Hannibal stared at the man for a moment and then asked, "You know what town it is?"

"I do," Fane said. "Friend of mine is the sheriff there, and I'm sure he's feeling pretty helpless right about now. That's why I like bein' the sheriff in a nothin' town like this. Ain't nobody in their right minds would want to take this town over."

"But your friend's town is a different story?" Hannibal asked.

"It's a growin' town—or it was until Walker Bogart and his came along."

"Why hasn't the word gotten out more?"

"Bogart and his men got everybody scared of them," Fane said. "People are just too darn scared to pass the word."

"How did you get the word?"

"My friend, Sheriff Ben Exman, managed to get one telegraph message to me when Bogart came into town. He was askin' for help, but I just didn't have enough men to make a difference."

Fane looked a little uncomfortable about admitting that. Hannibal had a feeling that Fane wasn't immune to a little fear himself.

"I see," Hannibal said. "Well, if you'd tell me the name of the town, we'll get over there and see what the situation is."

"How many men you got?"

"We're four."

"That ain't nearly enough men, Marshal Hannibal," Sheriff Fane said. "Not nearly enough to take on Bogart and his crew. If I was you *and* your friends I'd think twice about this."

"I appreciate that, Sheriff Fane, but there's a town that is practically being held hostage, and there's a friend of ours in there," Hannibal explained. "My friend and I aim to do what we can do to change that."

"Well," Fane said, "I warned you. When you leave town, ride for about five miles and you'll come to a turnoff. Take that turnoff and you'll be on it."

"On what?" Hannibal asked.

"On the road to Ceremony."

While Hannibal went to the sheriff's office, Maddux and Wilkes went to the hotel. Shadoweyes still had not put in an appearance since leaving the saloon that afternoon.

"What the hell happened to that Indian?" Wilkes asked when they were in their room.

"He's a big boy," Maddux said.

"What's that mean?"

"He can take care of himself."

"Okay. Then what's taking Hannibal so long?"

"Just relax, Wilkes," Maddux said. "They'll be along in time."

"Poker," Wilkes said derisively. "Three hours playing poker and what did you learn? That a couple of guys were cheating."

"I also made a few hundred dollars," Maddux said. "Not bad for three hours' work."

"A couple of hundred," Wilkes said. "We're dealing with fifteen thousand dollars here, and you're happy about a couple of hundred."

"Wilkes," Maddux said, "if we're both going to walk out of this room alive, you're going to have to change your tune."

"Is that a threat?"

"It's a suggestion, right now," Maddux said, "but I can make it a threat if you like."

They were facing each other when there was a knock on the door. Maddux walked to it, and opened it for John Shadoweyes.

"Did you find out anything?" Wilkes asked.

Shadoweyes stared at Wilkes, as if the other were speaking in a foreign language.

"Well?"

"Take it easy, Wilkes," Maddux said. "If he found out something he'll tell us."

"Yeah? And maybe he won't," Wilkes said. "Maybe he found out something and he's going to go after Bogart alone, and keep the reward. How about that?"

Maddux stared at Wilkes. "Is this the man who told me that partners should trust one another?"

"Yeah, well, it's plain that none of you want to be partners with me. Besides, he's an Indian. What's to keep him from running out on us?"

"If anyone was going to run out on the rest of us, Wilkes, my money would be on you."

"Hey, listen—"

"But I don't think any of us is going to run out," Maddux went on, "because no one of us would have a chance against Bogart alone."

Wilkes knew he was right, but wouldn't admit it.

"I found nothing," Shadoweyes said. "I asked questions and I listened to conversations, but I found nothing."

"Well," Maddux said, "maybe Hannibal has had some better luck."

On cue there was another knock at the door. Since Shadoweyes was standing in front of it, he simply turned and opened it, admitting Hannibal.

"I'm glad you're all here," Hannibal said. "I've got the answer." He clapped his hands when he spoke, and had an excited flush on his face.

"You know the name of the town?" Wilkes asked excitedly.

Hannibal looked at Maddux and said, "I know the name of the town and how to get there."

"The sheriff knew?" Maddux asked.

"He did. He was asked for help, but he said he didn't have enough men. I think he was just too . . . cautious to get involved."

"Come on, come on," Wilkes implored. "What's the name of the town?"

Still looking at Maddux, Hannibal said, "The town is called Ceremony."

Later Maddux and Hannibal were sitting in the saloon. Shadoweyes was off somewhere and Wilkes in his room at the hotel. They had decided to spend the night and get an early start for Ceremony the next morning.

"I have to say something," Hannibal said.

"So, say it."

"You're taking this very well."

"Taking what well?"

"The fact that Wilkes lied to you and lured you out of your retirement."

Maddux made a face at Hannibal and said, "Joe, I learned a long time ago nobody makes a bigger fool out of you than yourself."

"What's that mean?"

"I mean, maybe I was just looking for an excuse to make this trip, and Wilkes was it. Maybe he used me, but I used him as well."

"You mean you're not angry?"

"No," Maddux said. "I guess I feel a little foolish, but I'm not angry."

"But this trip hasn't even turned out to be the one

you wanted," Hannibal said. "We're going after Walker Bogart, not the Backshooter."

"Well," Maddux said, "maybe I'm thinking of that fifteen thousand dollars and what my end could mean to the ranch."

"You think if you return to Cromwell with almost four thousand dollars that Laura will forgive and forget?"

"Probably not," Maddux said. "Like we said before, Joe, there's not much we can do about the Backshooter until he claims another victim. In the meantime, we might as well go after Walker Bogart."

"Well," Hannibal said," I guess while we're in the neighborhood, it would be rude not to pay our respects, huh?"

Maddux smiled and said, "Yeah."

Thirty

Ben Exman didn't feel much like a sheriff in Ceremony anymore. In fact, he was surprised that Walker Bogart hadn't attempted to put his own man into his office by now. Maybe Bogart knew that the only way he'd be able to do that was over Exman's dead body. Up to now, Exman had taken his job very seriously. He'd been proud of the fact that he was the sheriff.

He wasn't so proud anymore.

He'd let Bogart and his men ride right into Ceremony, and right over everyone who lived here, including himself. That sure as well was not the action of a proud sheriff.

Exman, at thirty-five, had a combination of dedication and experience. His dedication told him to go out and face Bogart, but his experience told him that would be suicide.

Or maybe he was just frightened.

Well, sure he was frightened. He wouldn't be human if he wasn't, but he was also smart enough to know he couldn't do anything on his own. Early on he'd asked his friend, Sheriff Fane in Dennison, for help, but Fane had refused. Exman could understand that, couldn't hold it against the other man. If anyone died in defense of Ceremony it should be him, not a sheriff from somewhere else. There was no reason for the other man to volunteer to do that.

Exman had two deputies, and under normal circumstances they were good men, but they weren't stupid enough to commit suicide either.

If and when Ben Exman made a move, the conditions were going to have to be in his favor.

When that would be was anybody's guess.

Walker Bogart sat in the saloon, thinking about Anne Redman. He had given the woman plenty of time to come around—maybe *too* much time. He knew that his men were talking about him, and he was going to have to do something before some of them started to question him.

If that happened he might have to kill those men, and he had no desire to start killing his own men.

It made it hard to demand loyalty.

He didn't understand a woman like Anne Redman. He'd treated her fairly, he thought. Except for making her dress the way he wanted her to, he hadn't forced her to do anything.

Maybe tonight he was going to have to go over to the house and show Anne Redman what she'd been missing all this time.

Maybe it was time for him to show her who was whose captive.

Maybe it was time to just go over and rape the bitch and get it over with!

Thirty-One

"All right," Maddux said, "now that we finally know where we're going, we have to decide how we're going to play it."

"What do you mean how we're gonna play it?" Wilkes said. "We go in there and get Bogart, and collect our money."

"First of all," Maddux said, "do you know how many guns we'll be facing?"

Wilkes didn't answer.

"Do you?"

"No, I don't."

"Well, I don't either," Maddux said. "None of us do. And that's what we're going to have to find out before we do anything. Understand?"

"Sure," Wilkes said, "sure, I understand. I'm just a little . . . anxious."

Maddux looked at Hannibal and said, "Tell him what he gets for being a little anxious, Joe."

Hannibal looked at Wilkes and said, "Dead."

"Exactly," Maddux said. "You understand dead, don't you?"

"All right," Wilkes said, "you've made your point."

"I hope so," Maddux said. "All right, Joe or John, one of you have to ride in first. I can't because someone might recognize me, and obviously Wilkes can't because he's just not experienced enough."

"I'll go," Hannibal said.

"I will go," Shadoweyes said. Both men had spoken at the same time."

"We don't know how they will react to a stranger riding in, but John, I think if you ride in you might be more of a target."

"Because I am a half-breed?"

Maddux nodded. "That's like waving a red flag in front of a bull with some people. Some hardcase will see you and decide to try you just for something to do."

"So that means I go," Hannibal said.

That's the way I see it," Maddux said. "Anybody object?"

They all shook their heads.

"Anybody got a better idea?"

Again, they all indicated that they didn't.

"That's too bad," Maddux said. "I was hoping someone would."

"I'll ride on in in the morning," Hannibal said.

They had camped about an hour out of town so that whoever rode in could do so very early. The fewer people there were on the streets, the less chance there was of trouble.

"I suggest we all turn in," Maddux said. "Tomorrow's going to be a big day."

"Same watches?" Wilkes asked.

"Yeah, same watches."

Without further word Wilkes picked up his rifle and went to find himself a comfortable spot.

"Joe?"

"Yeah?"

Maddux held out his hand. "You'll have to leave the badge behind, just in case someone does challenge you. You might be searched."

Hannibal looked down at his shirt pocket, then took the badge out and held it in his hand. "I'll put it in my saddlebag."

"They might search that too," Maddux said. "Leave it with me. I'll take good care of it."

Hannibal looked down at it again and hefted it in his hand.

"All right," he said, handing it over, "but you better take good care of it. To some people it's just a piece of tin, but it means a lot more to me."

"I know it does," Maddux said, closing his hand over it. He tucked it into his own shirt pocket and said, "I'll take good care of it."

Hannibal nodded, then went to set up his bedroll.

"What about me?" Shadoweyes said.

"John, I think you should follow Hannibal to the edge of town. Keep an eye on his back trail. Wilkes and I will hang even further back. We'll have to give Hannibal enough time to ride in and get settled."

"And then what?"

"We can't all ride in," Maddux said. "Too many strangers on the same day might tip them off. Once Hannibal's inside, we'll have to find a way into town without being seen."

"After he is in, I will circle around and see if I can find a way in," Shadoweyes said.

"All right," Maddux said.

"Do we still watch Wilkes tonight?"

Maddux looked over to where Wilkes was sitting, then said, "Yes, tonight more than ever."

Thirty-Two

In the morning they all rose and had coffee. Over the fire they went over their "plan" once again.

"This doesn't sound all that well thought out to me," Wilkes said.

"Well now, if you've got a better idea I'd like to hear it," Maddux said. "That goes for anybody."

He looked around at all of them. Hannibal and Shadoweyes were looking at Wilkes, and Wilkes was finding something else—*anything* else—to look at.

"All right, then we'll go with what we've got," Maddux said.

Hannibal and Shadoweyes saddled the horses, and Hannibal mounted up first.

"Joe, you watch yourself when you get into town. Don't look crossways at anybody. The last thing we need is somebody to challenge you."

"Right. Good luck."

"To you too."

Hannibal rode off and Maddux turned to Shadoweyes. "Trail him, but stay well back."

"Right."

Shadoweyes mounted up.

"We'll be along behind you," Maddux told him.

"When I find a way in I will let you know."

"All right. Good luck, John."

After Shadoweyes rode off, Wilkes turned to Maddux and said, "What do *we* do now?"

Maddux turned to Wilkes and said, "Have another cup of coffee."

Hannibal rode down the main street of Ceremony, trying not to show the tension he was feeling. Maddux's temperament was probably better suited to this kind of subterfuge. Hannibal had not come out from behind his badge for a long time, and the experience was proving to be an eye-opener—with more to come.

Ceremony was different from the other towns they had ridden through. This town had the look of a place that was progressing. The buildings were all well cared for. Some of them were obviously new, and there were a few that were still in the process of being built—only no one was working on them at the moment.

Folks were probably just flat afraid to come out onto the street because of Bogart and his boys.

When he got to the livery he handed his horse over to an old man.

"Town's pretty quiet," he commented.

"Yep," the old man said.

"Something happen?"

"Nope," the man said. It was obvious that he wasn't going to say anymore than he had to.

"How long you stayin'?" the old man asked.

"Not long," Hannibal said. "Maybe just overnight. If I change my mind I'll let you know."

"You'll have to give me some money now," the old man said.

Hannibal dug into his pocket and gave the old man what he asked for.

"Saloon open this early?" he asked.

"The saloon is always open," the old man said, and walked the horse inside.

"I'll find it myself," Hannibal said to no one. Out of habit he reached up to touch the badge on his chest but it wasn't there.

Shadoweyes had trailed Hannibal right to the town limits and had stopped there. He looked for higher ground, found it, and was able to watch Hannibal ride into town. That done, he began to circle the town, looking for another way in.

Naturally, they could have entered from the other end, but that would still mean riding right down the center of the main street.

He circled the town completely twice, and could find only two other ways to enter. They could work their way down around behind the livery stable, or to an alley that ran right through from the main street to behind the general store.

He turned his horse and headed back to where Maddux and Wilkes would be waiting.

When Hannibal walked into the saloon there was no one there but the bartender.

"You serving beer this early?" Hannibal asked.

"I am if you're drinkin' it," the bartender said.

"Well, draw me one," Hannibal said.

The bartender drew a beer and put it in front of him.

"What's wrong with this town, anyway? It's real quiet," Hannibal said.

The bartender shrugged and said, "So it's quiet. A lot of towns are quiet."

"Not towns this size," Hannibal said.

"What are you, some kind of census-taker?" the bartender asked.

Hannibal realized then that maybe he was asking too many questions.

"No," Hannibal said, "I'm just a man looking for a beer and a meal."

"Well, you'll have to go down the street for the meal," the bartender said.

"As soon as I finish this beer, I'll do just that."

When Hannibal left the saloon, the bartender took off his apron and left also.

"Who is he?" Walker Bogart asked.

The bartender had gone to Walker Bogart's house to tell him the news.

"I don't know," the bartender said. "Just a stranger, I guess."

"So why bring him to my attention?"

The bartender shrugged. They were in the kitchen. Bogart had one of the saloon girls come in in the morning and make him breakfast, and when the food was ready he kicked her out and ate alone. He was drinking coffee now and did not offer the other man any.

"He was asking questions."

"About what?"

"About why the town was so quiet."

"What did you tell him?"

"I told him it was a quiet town."

"That satisfy him?"

"I guess."

Bogart thought a moment, then said, "All right.

Go back to work.''

The bartender nodded and left the house, and Bogart thought about what he'd said. From the way it sounded, the man was just a stranger riding through.

Still . . .

He finished his coffee and spent a moment thinking about Anne Redman. He had come back to the house last night drunk, with every intention of forcing himself on her. He'd been so drunk, however, that the flight of steps had looked miles long, so he had lain down on the sofa in the sitting room to rest.

That was where he'd awakened in the morning.

He hadn't even seen Anne Redman this morning. He'd had the girl from the saloon bring her breakfast up to her. His intention was to go up and see her after his own breakfast, but now there was this stranger to see to.

Maybe later.

Thirty-Three

Shadoweyes finished telling Maddux about the two alternate entry points he had found into town.

"Well, that's it," Wilkes said, "let's go."

"Just hold on a minute," Maddux said. "We've got to give Hannibal enough time to get the lay of things." He looked at Shadoweyes and asked, "How did the town look to you, John?"

"Quiet," Shadoweyes said, "much too quiet. I think perhaps the people are afraid to come out onto the street."

"Well, that's a possibility," Maddux said. "However, that can work for us or against us."

"How so?" Wilkes asked.

"Well, if there were people on the street we could blend in with them when we sneak into town."

"That's how it works against us," Wilkes said. "How does it work for us?"

"When the shooting starts," Maddux said, "we won't have to worry about hitting innocent bystanders."

Hannibal was eating in a small cafe when two

men entered. There were other diners in the cafe, and from their reaction he was sure one of the men was Walker Bogart. If he had to choose which one, he would have said the big one.

He continued eating, not looking at the two men. He didn't look up again until the two men positioned themselves right in front of his table. Behind them Hannibal saw several people scurry out of the cafe, leaving behind partially uneaten meals.

"Can I help you?" he asked.

"Not really," the big man said. "We're sort of the welcoming committee of Ceremony. You know, we like to make strangers welcome."

"Is that a fact?"

"Mind if I sit down?"

"I like to know who I'm sitting with."

"My name's Bogart, Walker Bogart. This here's Parnell."

"My name is Hannibal. Sit down a spell."

Bogart pulled out one chair and sat down. The other man, Parnell, remained standing.

"You boys want some coffee?" Hannibal offered. "I could get another cup."

"No, thanks," Bogart said. "You just passing through?"

"That's right."

"On your way to . . . where?"

Hannibal shrugged and said, "No place special." As an afterthought he added, "I'll just keep drifting until I find some work."

"Work, huh?" Bogart said. "What kind of work is it you do?"

Again Hannibal shrugged. "This and that."

Bogart leaned over and glanced at Hannibal's gun, but Hannibal didn't say anything. Bogart studied Hannibal a while longer in silence.

"Well," Bogart said, "we just wanted to make you feel welcome."

"You succeeded, Mr. Bogart. I thank you."

"Don't mention it."

Bogart stood up and he and Parnell walked to the door. Hannibal watched them, then finished his coffee, wondering what Bogart was thinking.

Outside Parnell said, "What do you think?"

"Did you see his shirt?"

"What about it?"

"On the left side, there were holes in it, small holes like a pin makes."

"So?"

"Pins," Bogart said, "the kind on the back of a badge."

"A badge?"

"Yeah," Bogart said, "what we got in there is a lawman."

"Maybe he used to be a lawman."

"Same thing," Bogart said. "Besides, that many fresh holes means that badge has been coming on and off a lot—and recently. No, he ain't no ex-lawman. He's a lawman."

"What are we gonna do?"

Bogart looked at Parnell and said, "What do we usually do with lawmen, Parnell?"

"Are we gonna wait until dark?" Wilkes asked.

"We can't," Maddux said. "I'd like to, but we can't leave Hannibal in there alone that long."

"Then when do we move?" Wilkes asked.

Maddux looked down at Ceremony, knowing that it was chock-full with Walker Bogart's men. "We might as well go now and get it over with."

"Well it's about time," Wilkes said.

"I just thought of something," Maddux said.

"What?" Shadoweyes asked.

"Look down there, both of you," Maddux said, pointing to the town.

"At what?" Wilkes asked.

"Just look at the town," Maddux said, "and imagine that you are Walker Bogart." He waited a moment, then asked, "You take what you want, right?"

"Right," Wilkes said.

"Where would you live?"

There was a moment of silence while both men thought about the question. Maddux wished he had thought of it before Hannibal had left.

"The hotel," Wilkes said.

"Use some imagination, Wilkes," Maddux said. "You can have any place you want. What would you take?"

"That saloon," Wilkes said. "I'd stay in the saloon with all the women."

"That house," Shadoweyes said, "at the far end of town."

"Why the house?" Maddux asked.

"Because it is the largest house in town."

"And would you keep a woman there, away from the other men?"

"Yes," Shadoweyes said, "if she's still alive."

"Yeah," Maddux said. "So would I. That's our first target."

"What about the saloon?"

"Forget about the saloon," Maddux said. "Shadoweyes, show us those two ways into town. We'll have to pick out the best one."

"Why don't we split up and go in both ways?" Wilkes asked.

Maddux stared at Wilkes and then said, "Wilkes, that's the first good idea you've had since we left."

Hannibal came out of the cafe and looked both ways. To his right a man stood, leaning against a post. He straightened up when Hannibal came out.

Well, they had sent a man to watch him. So much for his plan to lie back and listen like a fly on the wall.

Thirty-Four

Maddux decided to keep Wilkes with him, and let Shadoweyes go on alone. He and Wilkes would work their way around to the back of the livery stable and Shadoweyes would come down the alley. Once they made it to the livery stable they'd be about a block away from the house they had picked out as Bogart's.

Shadoweyes was to work his way down the alley, find a place to hide and wait. It wouldn't do to have Shadoweyes walking around town, attracting attention. He was going to have to hide and wait for all hell to break loose.

Maddux and Wilkes left their horses on high ground, tied to a stand of trees, and worked their way down behind the livery stable.

"What now?" Wilkes asked.

"I'll tell you what," Maddux said. "Sit tight here, the way Shadoweyes is doing in the alley, and wait until you hear from me—or until you hear a ruckus—then come running."

"And what are you gonna do?"

"I'm going to check that house and see if there's a woman being held there."

"Look, Maddux," Wilkes said, "don't forget why

we're here—"

"Your main concern is money," Maddux said, cutting him off. "Don't worry, Wilkes, you'll get what's coming to you. In fact, if everything goes right, maybe we'll both get what we want. Now stay here!"

Maddux moved away before Wilkes could argue.

Shadoweyes was in the alley, and there were some crates stacked against one wall. He pulled a crate away from the wall, and turned it around so that its open end fitted against the wall. He got inside the box, and inched it back against the wall so he was well hidden. He did not want to be found before the time came.

Maddux was surprised.

The town was even more deserted than it looked from outside. It seemed as if Bogart really had the entire town too scared to move.

He reached the big house and flattened himself against the wall on one side. He moved to the nearest window and peered in. He could see a sitting room, and there was a man with a rifle in the room. The excitement built inside him.

He'd found the woman. Why else would there be an armed man inside the house?

He moved around to the back of the house and looked in a window there. It was the kitchen, and there was a man sitting at a table eating. He had a rifle leaning against the table. There was no way Maddux could kick in the door, grab the rifle, and kill the man without the other man hearing it. He was going to have to find another way into the house.

He noticed that the kitchen stuck out from the rest of the house. He backed up and saw that the low roof gave access to the second floor. There was a barrel nearby, and if he stood on it he'd be able to reach the low roof and hoist himself up. He was going to have to wait for the man in the kitchen to finish and leave the room. There was no way he could walk on the roof without the man hearing him inside.

He flattened himself against the back wall of the house so that he could peek in the back window, and settled down to wait.

"What are we gonna do about the lawman?" Parnell asked.

"Dutrow is watching him, isn't he?"

"Yeah."

"So he can't do anything without us knowing about it."

"Why don't we just kill him?"

"Why don't *you* kill him?"

"Alone?"

Bogart regarded Parnell across the table, then picked up his beer and sipped from it. Parnell was a good lieutenant because he did what he was told, had never had a good idea of his own, and was a coward. There was no way he'd ever turn on Bogart.

"We'll kill him when I say so," Bogart said. "Let's see what the man wants first."

"How we gonna find that out?"

"Easy," Bogart said, smiling. "We're gonna ask him."

Hannibal had taken a turn around the whole town—the whole empty town—and his tail was still

191

with him. He was convinced that the man wasn't there to kill him, just to keep Bogart informed about him. Apparently, Walker Bogart had noticed something about him and wanted to be sure he knew his every move. There was no way of knowing what gave him away, but he was sure he'd find out soon enough.

Hannibal decided to go and get himself a hotel room. It was as likely a place to hole up as any while waiting for the fur to fly. Before long, Bogart would be coming for him, either to kill him or talk to him, find out what he wanted.

He hoped Maddux would move before then.

Long before then.

Maddux had one fear and that was that someone would move too soon.

He had worked with Hannibal for years now, and he knew Shadoweyes as a ranchhand, but he felt he could trust them when things got bad, and they hadn't shown him any different anywhere on the trail.

It was Wilkes he was most worried about.

If Wilkes panicked, he could get them all killed.

And Wilkes was as prime a candidate for panic as Maddux had ever seen.

As Maddux watched, the man in the kitchen finished eating, picked up his rifle, and left. Maddux waited a while to make sure the other man wouldn't come in for something to eat. When he was sure it was clear, he rolled the barrel over to the house, stood on it, reached up, grabbed the edge of the low roof, and pulled himself up onto it.

When he was on the roof he walked gingerly up to the nearest window. He looked inside the room and saw that it was a large bedroom. Best of all it was empty. He tried the window and found it unlocked. He slid it up and stepped into the room. He moved to the open door, stood still, and listened intently. He thought he could hear voices downstairs, but there was nothing up here.

He moved into the hall. Although he left his gun in his holster, he was prepared to draw it at any time. He moved quietly down the hall to a closed door and pressed his ear to it. He couldn't hear anything inside, so he turned the doorknob slowly and opened it.

The woman in the chair turned around and when she saw him her eyes widened in a mixture of shock, surprise . . . and utter joy.

"I don't know who you are, mister," the woman said, "but you're a dream come true."

Thirty-Five

Anne Redman rushed into Maddux's arms and he held her tightly. He was acutely aware of how much flesh was showing from what she was wearing—or what she was almost wearing.

"Was this the way he kept you from going outside?" he asked. "By dressing you like this?"

She shocked herself by laughing.

"This is how he kept me on display for him," she said, "but now that you mention it, I *would* be too embarrassed to go out like this."

"I hope not," he said, "because we're getting out of here now."

"I knew you'd come," she said, touching his face with both hands, "I knew it. By the way, who are you?"

"My name is Maddux."

"Well, Mr. Maddux, my name is Anne Redman and I can't thank you enough—"

"You can say thank you when we get away from here," he said, cutting her off.

"Away?" she said, backing up. "I don't want to get away."

Maddux was surprised. Had he made the wrong assumption here? "You what?"

"Not without Bogart."

"I don't—"

"I came here to get Bogart, Maddux," Anne said, "and after everything I've been through, I'm not leaving without him."

"You're a bounty hunter?" Maddux asked, finally catching on.

"What's the matter?" she demanded. "You never heard of a woman bounty hunter before?"

"No."

"Well, I am one, and I want Bogart. I'm not leaving without him."

Maddux studied her face and saw how deadly serious she was.

"Well," he said, "would you settle for his head on a platter?"

She smiled and said, "Yes!"

"Then we've got to get you some clothes."

"Hey!"

Anne Redman waited a moment, then called again.

"Hey, down there!"

When there was no reply she looked at Maddux.

"They're deciding who should come up," he whispered.

She shushed him when she heard someone coming up the steps.

"What the hell do you want this—" the man was saying, but he stopped short when he came into the room.

Anne Redman was naked to the waist, and the

196

sight of her just nailed him to the floor.

Maddux came out from behind the door and stuck his gun in the man's ear.

"Move and you're dead."

"I ain't movin'," the man said, and he still had not taken his eyes off Anne.

Maddux examined the man critically and said, "His clothes will never fit you."

"No," she said, "they'd be too small."

Indeed, the man was at least three or four inches shorter than she was.

Maddux screwed his gun deeper into the man's ear and relieved him of his gun.

"Call your friend," Maddux said, "and make it sound like there's something up here he's just got to see."

The man nodded. "Webb?"

No answer.

"Goddamnit, Webb! Get up here?"

"What the hell is it?" Webb called from downstairs.

"Come on up."

"What for?"

"Tell him . . ." Maddux said, whispering something in the man's ear.

"Webb . . . she's givin' it away up here."

Suddenly there was the sound of running feet on the steps. As the man called Webb ran into the room Maddux clubbed him over the head. Webb went sprawling onto the floor, and as the other man leaned over him, Maddux let him have it too.

"His clothes will fit you," Maddux said. "You might have to roll up the pants legs and the sleeves—"

"I'll roll them," Anne said. She bent over the man

and said, "Help me get him undressed."

"Right."

Maddux holstered his gun and reached for the man's shirt.

"You do the pants," Anne said.

"Right."

She started to unbutton the man's shirt, then looked at Maddux and repeated, "'She's givin' it away'?"

He grinned and said, "That would bring me running."

"All right," Bogart said to Parnell, "let's go and talk to our friend the lawman."

Hannibal looked out the window of his hotel room and saw Bogart and his man Parnell crossing the street from the saloon. He took out his gun and checked to make sure it was fully loaded, then opened the window.

When she was dressed, Anne took one of the men's gun belts and strapped it on.

"God," she said, "I feel dressed again."

"Yeah," Maddux said, "you looked dressed again too."

"Don't look so disappointed."

"Well, I kind of liked what you had on before." The comment surprised even *him*.

She smiled at him and said, "Why do I have this feeling that you're normally shy?"

"That was before I retired."

"Well, don't be so disappointed," she said. "Remember if we get out of this, I owe you my thanks."

Maddux wasn't sure what she meant, but he didn't pursue it. "Let's tie these yahoos up nice and tight and get to it, then."

Thirty-Six

"I have a plan," Maddux said.

"I knew you would," Anne Redman said. "I'm sure it's a well-thought-out, carefully mapped plan, with a safe escape and everything?"

"Well, actually I thought it up while we were undressing that fella upstairs."

They were standing at the front window of the house, looking out.

"What was it about that that gave you a plan?"

"Well, I noticed that his cuffs were frayed."

"And?"

"Well, who pays them so they can buy new shirts?"

"Bogart."

"And if Bogart was dead, who would pay him and the other men?"

"Nobody."

"Exactly."

"And that's your plan?"

"Yep."

"Would you like to explain it?"

"If we kill Bogart maybe the others will just . . . go away?"

Anne stared at Maddux for a moment, and then

said, "Maybe you've got something there. Why don't we go and try it out?"

"After you."

As they went out the front door she said, "Oh, I forgot to ask. Did you come alone?"

"No," he said, "I have three men with me."

"Only three?"

"Three," Maddux said again.

" Well, where are they?"

"They're strategically placed around town."

"How will they know when to move?"

"They'll know."

As they walked away from the house towards the main street—which Maddux noticed was called Front Street—Maddux said, "Oh, by the way."

"What?"

"You'll have to split the reward."

"With you?"

"With . . . everyone."

"Five ways?"

"I'm afraid so."

"Is the reward still fifteen thousand?"

"Last I heard."

"Well, three thousand is better than nothing."

"I hoped you'd look at it that way."

"Of course, it's too small a payment for what I've been through."

"Did he, uh . . ."

"No, he didn't," she said. "It was real strange. He put me in that house, dressed me, but never touched me. I couldn't figure it out."

"Maybe he just didn't know what to do with a lady," Maddux said.

"You didn't come here just to rescue me, did you?"

"No."

"You came for the reward?"

"No."

"Then . . . why *did* you come?"

"Bogart wanted me to."

"What?"

Maddux was about to make himself clearer when Anne hissed, "There he is!" She pointed. They moved out of the street and into a doorway.

Maddux saw two men crossing the street towards the hotel. "The big one?"

"Yes. What's that?"

"There?"

"Up there, on the hotel."

Maddux looked and saw a man climbing out a window. He recognized the bulk.

"That's Hannibal," Maddux said. "He's with us. Where are the rest of Bogart's men?"

"The hotel, the whorehouse—"

"How many does he have?"

"I don't know."

"I tell you what," Maddux said. "Let's go for Bogart without finding out."

"Why?"

"If we know for sure how many men he's got," Maddux said, "we might change our minds."

Hannibal watched until Bogart and Parnell were out of sight and then dropped down from the low roof outside his window. The man Bogart had watching him would still be in the lobby, and the three of them were probably now going upstairs to his room.

He started down the street and stopped when he saw someone up ahead.

"Maddux," he said to himself.

Maddux waved and Hannibal quickened his pace

and moved towards him.

"Who's this?" Hannibal asked.

"I'll introduce you later," Maddux said. "Get into the alley with Shadoweyes. Things are going to start jumping real soon."

"All right. Where will you be?"

Maddux looked around, saw the sheriff's office, and said, "In there."

"That reminds me," Hannibal said. "If I'm gonna die, I'd rather die with it on."

"Right," Maddux said, and handed Hannibal his badge.

"Luck," Hannibal said, and headed for the alley.

"Why the sheriff's office?" Anne asked.

"We can use the extra gun," Maddux said. "He'll be on our side."

Ben Exman stood up quickly as the door to his office slammed open.

"Who are you?" he demanded as a man and a woman entered. "Are you one of Bogart's—"

"We don't work for Bogart, Sheriff," Maddux said.

"Then who are you and what do you want?"

"We're here *for* Bogart, Sheriff."

"For the bounty on his head, you mean." Disdain was plain in the man's tone.

"For whatever reason we're here, it's your chance to be rid of him," Maddux said. "You can either help us, or watch us fight each other. If he wins, you're still under his thumb. If we win, I'll come back and kill you. The choice is yours."

Exman came around his desk and positioned himself in front of Maddux.

"I'll help you," Exman said, "but it's not because of any threat you made. I want my town back."

"Well then, let's go and get it."

Maddux started to turn and Exman put out his hand to stop him. "What's your name?"

"Maddux."

"How many of you are there?"

"Myself, the lady, and three others."

"When this is over, when we've taken the town back," Sheriff Ben Exman said, "I want you and your people out of it as fast as possible."

"Don't worry, Sheriff," Anne Redman said, "once I've done what I came to do, I won't be able to get out of this town fast enough."

Thirty-Seven

Wilkes looked in the windows of the house and saw that it was empty. More than ever he felt sure that Maddux had double-crossed him—maybe even double-crossed all of them—and had already taken Bogart out of town.

He moved away from the house and started walking down Front Street.

Maddux came out of the sheriff's office with the sheriff and Anne Redman.

"Sheriff, how many men does Bogart have?"

The lawman thought a moment before speaking. "You know something?" he said. "I don't know."

"How many have you ever seen at one time?"

"I always see Bogart and Parnell together, and at times I've seen Parnell with one or two other men."

"Does anybody know how many men Bogart has with him?" Maddux asked.

"I don't think so."

Maddux and Anne exchanged glances. She had only ever seen two men at a time, two pairs of them, who spelled each other staying at the house with her.

That made four men—Bogart, Parnell, and a couple of others the sheriff said he saw from time to time with Parnell.

Altogether, they had accounted for half a dozen men. Surely, Bogart had more than that with him.

"What are you thinking?" Exman asked.

"I'm thinking," Maddux said, "that Bogart may have taken this town by fear rather than by force."

"No, no," the sheriff said, "he must have an army with him."

"But no one's ever seen them," Maddux said.

"Still . . ."

"Look at the streets," Maddux said. "Your people are afraid to come out, but there should be some of Bogart's men around. They can't all be staying in the saloon, the hotel, and the whorehouse."

"So you're saying that there's just maybe half a dozen men?"

Maddux thought a moment, then said, "Yeah, that's what I'm saying."

"Hell, even if there's double that, we're not so outnumbered," Exman said.

"Do you have any deputies?"

"I do, but they haven't come around much since Bogart took over."

"All right, then it's the six of us," Maddux said. "Last I saw, Bogart was in the hotel."

"How do you want to handle this?" Exman asked.

"Head-on, I guess," Maddux said. "We'll face Bogart and see how many men come to his aid."

"Where are your men?"

"I've got two of them in an alley a block from here, and one back by the livery stable."

"Who's that?" Anne asked.

Maddux looked up and saw Wilkes walking down Front Street.

"He's one of mine," Maddux said. "I left him by

the livery. If Bogart sees him—"

"There's Bogart," Exman said, cutting off their conversation, "coming out of the hotel with Parnell and one other man."

"They'll see him for sure," Anne said, and even as she spoke they could tell Bogart and the two men with him had seen him.

"We'd better move . . . now!" Maddux said.

"I swear I don't know how he got out—" the third man was telling Bogart.

"Oh, shut up!" Bogart snapped.

"Walker," Parnell said, warningly, "another stranger."

"I see him."

"How'd he get into town?"

"It don't matter how," Bogart said. "That's two strangers in one day, and I don't believe in coincidence. Come on. Let's see what this one's got to say for himself."

Bogart stepped into the street and the other two men followed.

Wilkes saw the three men step into the street and panicked. He had heard and read physical descriptions of Bogart, and he knew that the big man in the center was the outlaw himself.

Wilkes drew his gun and fired, missing all three.

"Scatter!" Bogart shouted, drawing his gun. He fired at Wilkes, hitting him in the shoulder. The force of the bullet spun him around and deposited him on his butt in the center of the street. From that position Wilkes fired again, missing.

*　　　*　　　*

"That ass!" Maddux shouted.

"He's hit," Exman said.

"Give me some cover so I can get him."

"You've got it," Anne said.

She and the sheriff began to fire towards Bogart and his two men. Bogart, who had been taking a bead on the fallen Wilkes, turned toward the shooting, then turned again and dove for cover, as his two men had already done.

Maddux ran out into the street to grab Wilkes. At the same time three men came running from the saloon, two from the whorehouse, and two more from the hotel. They saw what was going on and drew their guns to fire at Maddux.

Hannibal and Shadoweyes came out of the alley, their guns drawn, to add cover for Maddux.

"What happened?" Wilkes asked as Maddux lifted him to his feet.

"You panicked, didn't you?" Maddux said.

"I—I—"

"Come on!"

He held the man around the waist and dragged him from the street to cover behind a horse trough.

"I'm dying!" Wilkes said.

Maddux checked his wound and saw that the bullet had struck him high on the right shoulder.

"You're not dying. Get up here, this is what you've been waiting for."

Wilkes struggled to his knees to look out over the trough.

"H-how many?" he asked.

"Near as I can figure, ten." Count the two he and Anne had left in the house, and that made a dozen. He hoped there wouldn't be more men putting in an appearance.

"That's all?" Wilkes asked.

"That's enough to take over a town," Maddux said. "Hell, two men could take a town if no one stands up to them."

The firing stopped and Maddux took stock of the situation. Down the street Bogart and his men had found cover in doorways, behind crates, inside storefronts.

Anne and the sheriff were in front of the sheriff's office, Hannibal and Shadoweyes had found some cover in doorways, and Maddux and Wilkes were behind the trough. Wilkes probably couldn't handle his rifle very well. He'd have to stay where he was and provide cover.

"Two to one odds," Maddux said. "Not bad, not nearly as bad as we expected."

"What do we do now?"

"I'd say we wait," Maddux said. "We just wait."

"How many you figure?" Parnell asked Bogart.

"Looks like six," Bogart said.

"How'd they get into town?"

"They walked right in," Bogart said, "while the men were drinkin' or whorin' or whatever they were doing." He looked at Parnell and said, "How many men we got?"

"Here and now?"

Bogart nodded.

"Ten."

"The woman is out, so that means that Webb and Carnes are probably dead."

"Ten to six," Parnell said. "I'd like it if the odds were even more in our favor. What do we do now?"

"Now we just wait," Bogart said.

Thirty-Eight

"What are they waiting for?" Wilkes said.

Maddux had torn some of Wilkes's own shirt off in order to use it to pack the shoulder wound.

"The same thing we're waiting for," Maddux said. "Someone to make the first move."

"Maybe they're waiting for the rest of their men?" Wilkes said.

"There are no more men, Wilkes," Maddux said. "If there were, they'd be here by now."

Maddux moved to the other end of the horse trough, and from there he could see Shadoweyes and Hannibal. He waved until they saw him, and then Maddux tried to convey his message through sign language. He couldn't see Anne or Exman from where he was, but he was sure Hannibal could. He hoped that he would pass on the message.

"What are they saying?" Exman asked. He could see Maddux's two men across the street, and one of them was waving at them.

"Up," Anne said.

"What?"

"Can I get to the roof of your office from inside?"

"No, you'd have to go to the back."

"Stay here," she said.

"Wait, what's going on?"

"I'm going to try to get above them. One of our men on the other side will do the same, and then we can fire down at them."

"Wait, wait," he said, "I'll climb up. I know how."

Anne studied the man for a moment, then said, "All right, but don't fire until Maddux does."

"Right."

Exman went inside his office and Anne waved to Hannibal that she understood.

Maddux waited until he saw Hannibal on one roof, and Hannibal waved that he saw either Anne or Exman on another roof.

"Stay here and provide cover," Maddux said.

"Where are you going?"

"I'm going to try and get closer and draw them out so we can get a better shot at them from the rooftops."

"I—I can't shoot," Wilkes said.

He'd been hit in the right shoulder, and he was right-handed.

"Shoot with the left hand."

"I can't hit anything left-handed."

"That's all right," Maddux said, "they don't know that."

Maddux got up into a crouch. "Get ready."

He took a deep breath and then ran out from behind cover.

"There he is!" Parnell shouted.

He stood up to fire and as he did most of the other

men stood up and fired also.

"No!" Bogart shouted, but it was too late.

When the firing started Bogart saw the two people on the rooftops. From above they had a clear shot at the standing men. He heard Parnell shout as a bullet struck him, and then several other cries of pain.

The odds were getting dangerously close to even, and that wasn't Walker Bogart's idea of odds at all.

Maddux fired on the run, striking one man. He ran diagonally across the street, his back screaming in protest, heading for a doorway. Shadoweyes came away from the buildings and fired, his bullets striking home at least once.

Maddux saw several of Bogart's men fall, and then he saw the big man shout something to his men before he started running.

Anne Redman came away from the sheriff's office firing, and also saw Bogart start to run.

He was trying to get away.

When Walker Bogart's men heard him shout, "Hold them off!" and saw him start running, they were confused. Some of them didn't hear what he said, they just saw him running, and if he was running, what were they staying there for?

Maddux, Shadoweyes, and Anne were advancing on the men, firing, and Hannibal and Exman were still firing from above, pausing only to reload.

Five of Bogart's men were down, three dead and two injured, and the other four lost their taste for the fight. They tossed out their guns and stood up with their hands high.

"This is the sheriff," Exman shouted from his

roof. "Just stand easy, men!"

Maddux, Shadoweyes, and Anne moved in and made sure the men were unarmed.

"Bogart," Anne said.

"I know," Maddux said, "I'll get him."

Maddux ran past everyone towards the livery. If Bogart had not bothered with a saddle he might be on a horse and out of town already.

Maddux stopped at the livery stable door and peered inside. His breathing was labored and he took a moment to close his eyes and breathe deeply. Damn, but he was too old for this!

He couldn't see Bogart, but he could hear him moving around. He was trying to saddle a horse, and the animal wouldn't stand still. It was probably spooked from all the shooting that had been going on.

"Stand still, damn it!" Bogart said.

Maddux stepped into the stable, gun in hand, and located the stall Bogart was in.

"Bogart!"

The big man turned and stared at Maddux. "Who are you?"

"I'm the man you've been waiting for," Maddux said.

"Maddux?"

"That's right."

Bogart turned away from the skittish horse and faced Maddux.

"I knew we'd end up like this," Bogart said.

"Take off your gun belt."

Bogart frowned. "This is man to man, Maddux. Holster your gun and let's get it over with."

"Don't be a fool!" Maddux said. "This is not some contest between us. I'm taking you in."

"For what? The bounty?"

216

"No, not the bounty."

"I didn't think so." Bogart said. "That doesn't mean anything to men like you and me."

"Don't put me in with you, Bogart. We're nothing alike."

He could tell from the look on Bogart's face that the man was disappointed.

"Maddux—"

"Come on," Maddux said, "drop the gun belt and let's go."

"You're not taking me in, Maddux."

"You're right," Maddux said. "Anne Redman is taking you in."

"The woman?"

"That's right," Maddux said. "You're her meat."

"I'm not a hunk of meat!"

"With that bounty on your head that's just what you are, a high-priced hunk of meat."

"I'll show you—" Bogart said, his hand moving for his gun.

"Don't!" Maddux said, but the man didn't stop.

Maddux ran towards Bogart, throwing the man off balance. Bogart tried to back away, his hand still clawing for his gun, and Maddux hit him on the jaw with the butt of his gun. Bogart staggered backward, his arms windmilling as he tried to stay on his feet. Finally he fell heavily to the ground, sticking out his left hand to break his fall. Maddux heard a bone in that hand crack.

Jesus, he thought, they break the law, they kill without a thought, and when their time comes they think they're entitled to some kind of a fair fight.

If Maddux fought fair he'd have been dead long ago.

Maddux started to approach Bogart when he saw that the fight hadn't gone out of the man. Bogart,

217

still supporting his weight with his injured hand, had drawn his gun.

"Shit!" Maddux said.

He raised his gun and fired. His bullet struck Bogart just above the right eye. The gun in Bogart's hand discharged once harmlessly, and then the man fell over, dead.

Epilogue

After they delivered Walker Bogart and his men to the law Maddux, Hannibal, and Shadoweyes planned to head back to Cromwell. They would leave Wilkes behind to be patched up and go his own way. Maddux handed Wilkes his share of the bounty—three thousand dollars—and then charged him fifteen hundred for the job.

"Fifteen hundred!" Wilkes screeched.

"Maybe this will teach you to be more straight-forward next time you need somebody's help—and take my advice, Wilkes."

"What's that?"

"You'd better stick with what you know from now on, Wilkes," Maddux said.

"What I know is spending money," he said, "and you aren't leaving me a whole lot to spend."

Maddux smiled and said, "Spend it slowly—after you pay me my fee."

Wilkes grudgingly paid the money.

"Fifteen hundred dollars and a bullet in the shoulder," he muttered as Maddux left his room. "Don't seem near enough."

"I know," Maddux said, before going out the door,

"think about it."

Anne Redman also parted company with them in Ceremony. When Anne was saddling her horse to leave, Maddux entered the livery stable and handed her an envelope.

"What's this?" she asked.

"That's the fifteen hundred I charged Wilkes," he said. "It's yours."

"I got my share, Maddux," she said, pushing the envelope away.

"You didn't get nearly enough to make up for what you went through, Anne," he said. "Bogart was your bounty to begin with."

"The bounty is anyone's," she said. "You and others earned your shares."

"This is not my share," he said. "This is what I swindled Wilkes out of. Believe me, he had it coming."

"I don't doubt it."

She stared at the envelope, then took it and said, "All right. Thanks."

They heard footsteps approaching, and were joined by Shadoweyes and Joe Hannibal.

"I was hoping I'd be in time to say good-bye," Hannibal said to Anne. It had been clear to Maddux from the moment Hannibal met Anne Redman that he was smitten.

"You are," she said, and gave the hulking marshal a hug that made him blush.

"I don't know if I can ever thank you all for what you did," she said, looking at them all.

"You have," Maddux said.

She stepped to Maddux and surprised him by kissing him quickly on the mouth.

She mounted up, waved, and rode off without looking back.

"That's a fine woman," Hannibal said.

"Yes, she is," Maddux said, "and a good new friend to have."

"What is it about you in your old age that attracts younger women?" Hannibal asked.

Maddux ignored the remark.

"It's too bad you had to kill Bogart," Hannibal said.

"I tried not to."

"I'm sure you did," Hannibal said. "It must be hell not knowing why he chose you."

"Chose me?"

"Sure," Hannibal said. "There are other reputations he could have gone after. Why did he pick you?"

"You mean you think that the attempts on my life in Cromwell had nothing to do with Wilkes coming there?" Maddux asked.

"As much as I know you hate coincidence," Hannibal said, "that's what I think. Wilkes or no Wilkes, I think Bogart had decided to try and lure you out of retirement, one way or another. If his men had killed you, then he'd go after someone else's rep, but you killed two of them and found out from the third that Bogart had sent them. Without Wilkes's deal, wouldn't that have been enough to draw you out?"

"You know it would have," Maddux said. "You know if you're right, then I've got more of an answer than I ever thought I'd have. Thanks, Joe."

"Well," Hannibal said, "some of us are put on this earth to—"

"I have your money right here," Maddux said, interrupting his pontificating friend.

"I told you, I don't want it," Hannibal said.

"Joe—"

"Did Shadoweyes take his?"

"No," Maddux admitted. "He told me to invest it in the ranch, so now we're partners."

"Well," Hannibal said, thoughtfully, "if you can stand another partner, you can do the same with mine. Nine thousand dollars would go a long way towards putting the place on its feet."

"On its feet?" Maddux said. "For that much money we could have us one damned fine horse ranch . . . partner."

Hannibal grinned, and a handshake sealed the deal.

"Where do we head now?" Hannibal asked.

"Now," Maddux said, "we go home."

"What about the Backshooter?" Hannibal asked. "I mean, he's the reason you started all of this."

"No," Maddux said, "I'm the reason. I was chafing at the bit while retired, but this whole experience had shown me that retirement isn't half bad."

"Then . . . you're just going to forget about him? About him killing twelve people?"

"There have been a lot of killers over the years that I couldn't do anything about, Joe," Maddux said. "This has to be just one more. This is a bad one for me to have to ignore, because of the way he kills, because I know what that feels like, but believe me, I'm going to do my best to try. Right now all I want to do is go home and see if Laura will have me back."

"Well, the man may be finished," the marshal of Cromwell said. "Twelve may have been his number."

"And now he'll disappear from sight and never be heard from again?" Maddux said.

"It's possible," Hannibal said. "I read about this killer in England who cut up a bunch of women, killing them, and then just stopped and disappeared."

Maddux took a moment to consider that possibility. He didn't like it any better than he liked walking away from the hunt. The thought that the man might get away with twelve murders didn't sit right with him.

Shadoweyes chose that moment to speak his piece. "Justice will find him," he said.

"What?" Hannibal said.

"Not your kind of justice, my friend," Shadoweyes went on, "but the kind that finds us all."